ANCHORS
AWEIGH

ANCHORS AWEIGH

VOYAGE TO WHAT I CHOSE TO BECOME

ALBERT SCHRIBER

ANCHORS AWEIGH
VOYAGE TO WHAT I CHOSE TO BECOME

Certain characters in this work are historical figures, and certain events portrayed did take place. However, this is a work of fiction. All of the other characters, names, and events as well as all places, incidents, organizations, and dialogue in this novel are either the products of the author's imagination or are used fictitiously.

iUniverse books may be ordered through booksellers or by contacting:

iUniverse
1663 Liberty Drive
Bloomington, IN 47403
www.iuniverse.com
1-800-Authors (1-800-288-4677)

Because of the dynamic nature of the Internet, any web addresses or links contained in this book may have changed since publication and may no longer be valid. The views expressed in this work are solely those of the author and do not necessarily reflect the views of the publisher, and the publisher hereby disclaims any responsibility for them.

Any people depicted in stock imagery provided by Thinkstock are models, and such images are being used for illustrative purposes only. Certain stock imagery © Thinkstock.

ISBN: 978-1-4917-5089-6 (sc)
ISBN: 978-1-4917-5090-2 (e)

Printed in the United States of America.

iUniverse rev. date: 01/21/2015

Edited by Wayne H. Purdin

TABLE OF CONTENTS

"I am not what happened to me, I am
what I choose to become."

– Carl Jung

"You must have chaos within you to
give birth to a dancing star."

– Friedrich Nietzsche

GEIGER

I hated my stepfather, Geiger, so much, I would dream about killing him. One night, I dreamt that I drove to his house in Metairie, Louisiana and went to the side of the house where there was a deep hole in the ground that looked like the beginning of a swimming pool. I noticed at the shallower end, my brother James with three other workers were still digging the hole. Geiger was on the far side standing over the deep end of the pool, drunk as usual, when he saw me looking toward him, he slipped and fell into the deep end that had some water in it. There was a front-end loader near the deep end and a pile of dirt that had been dug out. I jumped on the front-end loader and started burying him alive. I was pissed when I woke up and realized it was just a dream.

Geiger was born in Picayune, Mississippi and could have been the poster boy for abusive, alcoholic, red-necked sons-of-bitches. His abusive behavior toward my mother and sister surpassed anything a person should expect to suffer in a lifetime. My mother died of cancer at the early age of fifty-six, although it could have been said she died of a broken heart. My sister was sent to Acadia Baptist Academy (ABA), a boarding school in Eunice, Louisiana to get away from Geiger. Many times, I wished my mother would permanently move away from Geiger, but when she didn't, I moved to Baton Rouge, Louisiana to live with my father to escape this horrible environment at the age of fifteen.

When I lived with my mother and Geiger, there were very few pleasant times. Geiger was constantly drunk without any capacity to reason. Sundays and holidays often became nightmares for us because he drank more heavily on these occasions, and the more he drank, the more evil he became toward us. He would walk around the house cursing and banging on the locked bedroom door where we were hiding. Then he would sit in his overstuffed chair, chain smoking his unfiltered Camel cigarettes as the smell of cigarette smoke and stale beer filled the air. I was so afraid of his yelling, that sometimes, I would bury myself in a dark closet to muffle the noise.

I witnessed my mother's constant abuse and humiliation for many years. I felt helpless and wished I had the ability stop Geiger or maybe kill him. I believed there were probably a number of reasons I could do it, but I liked watching Baretta, and every episode began with a song that warned, "Don't do the crime if you can't do the time." I knew deep down in my soul that incarceration would not be good for me.

I loved my mother and wanted more than anything to experience a loving relationship with her. But she was stuck in a dark world of abuse. I could never understand why she would decide to break away from Geiger then, within months, she would go back to him. I assumed her prescription drugs were her only escape from the harsh reality of her life. After her early death, I discovered that her doctor prescribed barbiturates and methamphetamines, which may have contributed to her death. I never did develop the close relationship with her that I wanted.

My mother married Geiger when I started junior high school until the start of high school; I despised every minute I lived with him. As anticipated, living with my father in Baton Rouge didn't work out. I was a loner, went to school during the week, and played golf by myself on the weekend. I was treated like an outsider by classmates at school and by my stepmother at home, which depressed me. During my sophomore year, my mother and I moved to Crowley, Louisiana to escape Geiger and be close to my sister in Eunice. After Crowley, my mother had moved back with Geiger and wanted me to move back too, but I said, "No way, impossible." I was glad I was able to convince my mother to allow me to live in an apartment several blocks away on my own. With her financial help and my part-time job, I would be able work and go to school without living with Geiger.

During my senior year, when I was working as a welder, I summonsed the courage to visit my mother on Christina Street. When I entered Geiger's house to talk with my mother, I found her crying, naked, and covered with blood, lying on the floor in her bedroom. I covered her with a blanket then called the operator to request police and an ambulance. I said to myself, "That is enough; that's his ass." Geiger was over six feet tall and weighed two hundred and twenty pounds; I was one hundred forty-five pounds tops, but during the last two years, I had practiced Judo; therefore, I was ready. Within a few minutes, Geiger pulled into the driveway and entered the house with a brown grocery bag filled with beer. I angrily confronted him, then, with a powerful leg sweep, I put him flat on his back on the kitchen floor. Geiger's head bounced off the tile floor then I punched him in the face and neck as hard and fast as I could until he wasn't moving anymore. The force of my punches broke my senior ring and knocked Geiger's false teeth out of his mouth. A loud bang on the front door startled me as the police entered the kitchen with their weapons drawn and pointed at me. I had come so close to killing the bastard, but I wept because I witnessed my mother's unconscious body being wheeled on a stretcher to the waiting ambulance. She survived this brutal episode, but Geiger would recover to finish the battle.

THE PREACHER'S DAUGHTERS

Preacher's Daughter Syndrome is *"An affliction (usually affecting young females, though some U.S. politicians have confirmed cases) that is the result of overprotective, usually Christian upbringing. Due to being taught that everything is sinful, upon reaching the age of puberty and learning of unwholesome activities for the first time, sufferers have no common sense on the issue. This results in sexual promiscuity, drug dependence, shallow personality, and other personality defects."*
(Urban Dictionary)

When my mother and I moved to Crowley, I was glad to be close to Eunice, Louisiana, so I could visit my sister, Jan at ABA more often. ABA was an all-girl's boarding school for troubled teens and the lovely students were not allowed to leave the campus. I would later learn that these "lovely" girls' behavior could be likened more to one of Freud's dreams.

I was enrolled in the only high school in Crowley, which was only six or seven blocks from the house that my mother rented. I walked to and from school each day and had a newspaper route in the early morning to make extra money for our tight budget. My mother bought me a new black Schwinn bicycle, which I only rode for my paper route. The local newspaper was so thin, the paperboys had to fold and tuck them into a tight square form; this helped us hold multiple papers and toss them onto the customers' driveways or porches. Crowley only had two main roads in and out of the town square and most everyone lived within a couple of miles of the square; this made it easy for me to quickly learn my paper route. But I still got turned around sometimes because my route was before the sun came up in the morning.

All good citizens went to church on Sunday; besides, there wasn't any other social event, except the tradition of parading the town circle, which was practiced in the afternoon on Sunday. Crowley only had two churches: a Catholic one and a Baptist one. The largest percent of the population in Louisiana, especially the Acadian population, were diehard Catholics, but that did not stop the "bible thumping" Baptist from their evangelizing to frighten their evil cathartic souls. I was raised Catholic just like my father and grandparents, but I talked my mother into going to the Baptist church because I wanted to check out the stories and rumors I had heard about the preacher's daughters. They attended the same high school, and I didn't know them from Eve, but from the rumors, they were as seductive as

Eve. When we arrived at the Baptist church, the preacher, his wife, and their two daughters were standing in front of the church, greeting the members and their guests. I noticed the sisters were close to my age, fifteen or sixteen. Gail was the younger sister with pretty red hair and fair complexion, and Linda was older with light brown hair and more tanned. Both were slim and shapely girls. They were not gorgeous, but they had a certain sexy magnetism to their personality; they appeared to have been taught the art of seduction because they knew how to present themselves. Needless to say, I could not take my eyes off of them and planned to pursue getting to know them better somehow.

Weeks passed without any opportunities to meet the preacher's daughters; there weren't any new rumors or stories either. But one afternoon, as I walked home from school, Gail and Linda followed me to my house. I was shocked to see both of them standing there but was glad.

"Hi, Joseph, so, you're new to the high school," Linda said.

"Yeah, my mom and I moved here about a month ago from New Orleans because my sister goes to ABA." I lied because I didn't want to tell them the real reason.

"Gail and I are sisters and we—"

"Yeah, I know who you are," I interrupted. "I went to your church a couple of Sundays ago."

"Then you know the pastor is our father."

"Yeah, um, yeah, I do. Is that a problem for you?"

Linda ignored my silly question and got down to business. "We wanted to invite you to our Harvest Festival next week. There will be a teen program at the church, then, following that, all of the teens are going on a hayride."

Now, I had heard of a hayride, but I was unaware that teens actually went on hayrides. I also knew that fundamentalists didn't celebrate Halloween because they believed it was evil with all the kids dressing up like devils, witches, and monsters. I had a bad experience at a Baptist church in New Orleans and I didn't want to get involved with Baptist zealots again, but I did want to get to know Linda and Gail, so I decided to be noncommittal.

"Well, I guess so, maybe..."

"You don't have to decide now, but..."

I decided to skip the teen program then showed up just in time for the hayride. The hayride started right before sunset with only eight boys, and twelve girls. I liked the odds, but I soon learned I was not as savvy as I thought I was. The hay wagon rolled along the pothole-filled country road as the sun set and the evening became as dark as being locked in a closet, except for the dim moonlight. I noticed that many of the teens started to hide themselves in the piles of straw. Linda and Gail tag-teamed me for most of the night, not much conversation, mostly kissing and being immature teenagers.

Halloween passed, then Thanksgiving. My mother and I moved back to New Orleans before I had a chance to say goodbye to the preacher's daughters.

THE DRAFT

"On December 1, 1969, the Selective Service System of the United States conducted two lotteries to determine the order of call to military service in the Vietnam War for men born from 1944 to 1950. The draft occurred during a period of conscription in the United States, controlled by the President, from just before World War II to 1973. The Selective Service System commonly uses the label 1970 or says "Issued 1969 – Applied 1970". These lottery numbers were used during calendar year 1970 both to call for induction and to call for physical examination, a preliminary call covering more men." (From Wikipedia)

It was just after Christmas of 1968. My brother-in-law James and I had just finished having lunch and playing the All Stars pinball machine (the only cash payoff machine around) at "The Comeback Inn" in Metairie when James pulled out a letter he received and handed it to me.

"I got this in the mail yesterday, Joe," he said with a worried look on his face. "Please tell me I can get out of it."

I read the letter. It was a draft notice. James was three years older than me and a lot more "laid-back." His easy-going nature went well with my edginess, so I liked James and was happy that my sister had a good-natured, level-headed husband to care for her. He was like the big protective brother I never had. But this time, I was the one calming him down. I knew I would miss him and I was starting to choke up. But I swallowed and decided to make light of it. I handed the letter back, saying, "James, you didn't win at pinball, but you won the draft lottery. This is your induction notice for the Army.

"But I didn't get that first notice they talked about!

"Well, you'll have to report anyway."

"What am I going to do?"

"Not much you can do. You have to report as ordered, soldier." I said with a chuckle even though I wanted to hug him and tell him how much I was going to miss him. I knew if I did that, I wouldn't be able to keep from getting all teary-eyed. Instead, I just elbowed him in the ribs.

James was drafted into the Army, and, since he didn't report for the first notice, he was sent to Army boot camp at Fort Polk, Louisiana. A couple of weeks later, James wrote to me about some of the horrors of Army boot camp: the forced marches in the blistering sun, exhausting obstacle courses, and insane drill Sergeants. I didn't want to wait for the next draft in December 1969 and be sent to Army boot camp and then to the rice paddies of Vietnam, so I planned to join the Navy in April.

After boot camp, James wrote to me again and told me that it worked out fine for him. He volunteered to go to Korean and serve as a Preventive Medicine Specialist (PMS) for thirteen months. He was able to get this cushy position because he knew a few things about pharmaceuticals from working part-time at several drug stores.

Then, when he got to Korea, he wrote again, making me jealous. He said the first person he got acquainted with was "Queenie." Queenie was well known as "a mature lady of the evening." She was the madam for the local prostitutes. James learned his assignment as a PMS included inspection of the local restaurants for food safety and checking that the prostitutes had their health cards. No doubt, the cooks at the restaurants curried his favor with free samples of their food, and I wondered about the prostitutes. James even had a "tent boy" who cleaned the tent, his uniform, and shoes for only a few dollars a month.

James had me thinking that maybe the Army wasn't that bad after all, and that maybe I could get a cushy job too. But I didn't want to push my luck. Besides, I was a Navy man at heart.

THE CUSTOM HOUSE

In February of 1969, I got my own letter in the mail, an "Order to Report for Physical Exam," which was the preliminary step to being selected for the draft. I was requested to appear the following month at the Custom House on Canal Street in New Orleans for a physical exam and the Armed Forces Entrance Exam. I had to read it carefully several times because it was written in bureaucratese. I realizing that, if I didn't do well on the exam, there was a good chance I would be inducted into the Army. I decided to report as directed and take my chances, but I could kick myself for not enlisting in the Navy sooner. The month went by too fast, and it wasn't because February only had twenty-eight days.

I knew where the Custom House was located on Canal Street because I had passed it many times during Mardi Gras and visits to Cafe Du Monde in the French Quarter for coffee and beignets. As I drove down Canal Street, I flashed back to some fond memories of having fun at the Mardi Gras with James. This didn't stop me from feeling anxious because I wasn't sure what to expect at all, especially after reading the stories James told me about the Army. I parked my car on a lot on Poydras Street near Mother's Restaurant and walked several blocks to the location on Canal. I was hoping to finish the exam and physical early so I could get a "Ferdi Poboy Special" at Mother's for lunch. Words just can't describe the goodness of their poboys. It's a huge piece of French bread stuffed with baked ham, roast beef, debris, some mustard, and, to top it all off, gravy soaking the entire sandwich.

When I entered the building, there was a huge hallway with locations for many offices. I wasn't sure where I was supposed to report, so I walked over to the information desk near the middle of the building to ask for directions to the Armed Forces Examination office. A marine in a starched dress uniform pointed to the induction office located toward the back of the building. I thanked him and walked into the crowded office. I couldn't believe how many draftees were there, I estimated that there were over one hundred men sitting in rows of chairs. Now, if could just get examined first, there was still a chance I could have my poboy at Mother's.

A Yeoman First Class came to the front of the group and announced that all of us would take the Armed Forces Entrance Exam and induction physical. These tests would determine our suitability and placement in the armed forces. The yeoman split us into two groups: one group would take the entrance exam first and the other group would start with the physical. I was selected to take the physical first.

Now, I had been to a doctor for a checkup before, but this room was nothing like the doctor's office. The area was a large, drafty, and dreary room with few decorations and several smaller areas with ugly curtains, and the bare walls were lined with drab cabinets filled with stripped-down medical supplies. I was in the first batch of twenty men to get prepped for the examination. We were ordered to sit on the benches in the center of the room and remove all of our clothes, except for our underwear, then form a line shoulder-to-shoulder. The doctor and his assistant started at the left end of the long line; they checked each person with a stethoscope as they moved down the line. Damn that stethoscope was cold! After this initial screening, we were told to remove our underwear. It is an creepy feeling being naked in a room full of other naked men. Then, the doctor went back down the line, asking each man to turn his head and cough as he held their balls in his hand. He threated to crush the balls of any man who failed to turn his head and coughed in the doctor's direction. From the way he said it, I was certain he would carry out the threat. The doctor finished checking for hernias, then the next command was a surprise to everyone—bend over and spread your cheeks. All but one person followed the instructions by bending forward from the waist and spreading their butt cheeks with each hand for the doctor to check for hemorrhoids. To everyone's amusement, one large man at the end of the line, who looked like a jock, had both his index fingers in his mouth spreading his other cheeks. I thought that he wouldn't do well in the written exam either and would be going into the Army for sure.

I was a little nervous about the rectal exam because when I was fifteen, I had a bad case of hemorrhoids. I had tried to use suppositories and witch hazel to cure it, but it just wouldn't go away. So finally, I told my mother about it, who scheduled an appointment with a doctor, which turned out to be somewhat of an embarrassment and a pain in the ass, literally, for me. After the doctor checked me, he gave me several shots of medicine directly in my tender rectum. The doctor told me that the shots would be the worse part, and he was right, except he didn't tell me that my butt-hole would feel as wide as the opening to the Harvey tunnel. It took several weeks before I had a normal bowel movement again.

Fortunately, at the induction physical, I only had a minor case of hemorrhoids and marginal high blood pressure, so I passed with flying colors, unlike some other guys. I couldn't believe that so many young men could pass, even after testing positive for marijuana and having heart or kidney problems or some other physical ailment. I guess the physical requirements for passing were pretty low by any standard. There were even several men with orange coloring in their urine who passed the physical. I wondered how they could ever survive boot camp if they were so out of shape. I felt sorry for them.

Next, I took the Armed Forces Entrance Exam. The test was mostly math and logic questions with multiple-choice selections for answers. My strong points were math and reasoning and I was good at taking tests. Being multiple-choice only make it easier for me. So I finished ahead of time and felt happy with the test. It was implied that to get into the Army or Marines, you only needed to score forty out of eighty points. You were probably given forty points just for getting your name and home address correct. I was confident that I had aced the test as I waited in the adjacent room for the results.

The other recruits weren't so confident and asked each other if they got some of the harder questions. Everyone became silent when the proctor came back in with the results. All exams were returned to the test takers and they were dismissed with the exception of three men: the jock, another stupid-looking guy, and me. The first two flunked the exam and were asked to step into another room. I could believe I flunked. Maybe my test was mixed up with someone else's. Then the proctor sat next to me and stared at me oddly for a second before asking, "Okay kid, how did you cheat on the test? Did you get ahold of the answers from someone?"

I was shocked. I had never been accused of cheating before. I was also insulted and angry. My blood started to boil, but I made sure my voice and face didn't show any feeling other than surprise when I answered, "What? No, I didn't cheat. Why do you think I cheated?"

The proctor didn't look like he believed me. He sighed and said, "Look, kid, you got a seventy-six. You only missed one question. That's not possible to do without cheating. So tell me how you did it."

"No, I swear. I didn't cheat. I'm just really good at math and reasoning. I can show you."

"Okay, show me how you solved this problem," the proctor asked, pointing to one of the hardest questions.

It was a quadratic equation problem. I showed him how I did it, balancing the sides and solving for x. But this didn't seem to satisfy him.

"Okay, so you know how to solve those problems, but maybe someone coached you who knew how to do all the problems on this exam. I'm sorry, but you'll have to take another exam today.

I felt like saying, "Screw you" and walking out, but that would result in a fast ticket to Army boot camp. So I obediently took the new exam, passed that exam as well, and scored high enough to get into the Navy. I still can't figure out what the issue was that day. The proctor was an Army corporal; maybe he wanted me for the Army. I was also annoyed that I never made it Mother's Restaurant for my poboy because the exam took too long.

THE WELDER

Before leaving for boot camp, I spent the summer with my grandparents in Harahan, Louisiana and worked as a welder for a Navy contractor that made metal parts for the twenty-six destroyer escorts being built at Avondale shipyards across the Mississippi river. The owner and brains of the business was Curtis, a rugged-looking man, but one with a heart of gold. I had learned to weld during a class in high school shop, so I started as one of the tack welders, assembling the flanges onto the metal spools by spot welding the pieces.

Curtis always came by the outside welding table to check on the progress and helped me to become a better welder; thus I became an excellent welder in a very short time. I even became very efficient in welding aluminum, which was considered to be a difficult process. In less than a month, my skills improved to the level where I could become a MIG (metal inert gas) welder. The MIG welding station was inside a large metal building in the center of the yard. My job was to finish welding the "tacked spools" and then use a metal grinder to smooth the welded joint. Curtis invented a circular metal table that turned at a slow speed to help facilitate the welding of the spools; this made the welding process fast and even decreased the welding errors. I really liked doing this type of welding and was able to produce more work than most of the more experienced welders.

It was summer so the heat was nearly unbearable inside the building. Some of the older, out-of-shape welders had to take frequent breaks, but I was able to continue welding throughout the day without stopping, except for lunch. I only weighed about one hundred and forty-five pounds, but for lunch, I was able to eat three Burger King Whoppers, a large order of fries, a chocolate milkshake, and two small apple pies without gaining any weight. I didn't know it at the time, but my eating habits would not last forever.

I continued working for Curtis until the time came for me to leave for boot camp. I would fondly remember my summer welding job, the skillful tutoring I received from Curtis, but, most of all, I would always cherish his kindness. Curtis was the first male figure in my life that didn't abuse me.

BOOT CAMP

"The real fun begins when you are assigned a Recruit Division Commander (RDC) and get to meet your instructor. Addressing an RDC as "Sir," warrants the death penalty. It's vital that you address a Chief as "Chief so-and-so." Navy RDCs' are hard-of-hearing, and you'll have to yell at them in order to be heard. Navy Chiefs wait with eager anticipation for new recruits to address them as "sir," This is normally followed by a tyrannical display, intending to throw recruits into a total disarray of confusion, while demonstrating that it is really Navy Chiefs who are in charge of the Navy."
(Unknown)

I was as green a recruit as any eighteen-year-old or more so when I arrived in early August at NAS San Diego, ready for my boot camp training for three months of indoctrination into the U.S. Navy. My father and uncle were both sailors in World War II, but I didn't have the slightest idea of what to expect in training, since they never talked about their experiences in the Navy. All I knew was from watching television and listening to stories from other people. I was never sure what was true or what was dramatization or exaggeration. After our company of eighty new recruits arrived on buses that evening, we were processed through indoctrination, issued all of our uniforms, taken to our barracks, and instructed to bed down for the night. Before going to sleep, I chatted with my bunkmate, Bob, who was from Texarkana, Texas, close to home. He was also smart, so we had a lot in common. Bob helped lessen the feeling of homesickness that had been bothering me ever since I left Metairie.

"I'm so glad I was able to get in the Navy," I told Bob. "My brother-in-law was drafted in the Army, and he told me some horror stories about Army boot camp."

Little did I know that in the next month, we were about to receive more abuse and humiliation than we would ever experience in a lifetime. I was from a dysfunctional family with an alcoholic stepfather and a prescription-drugged mother. I thought it would be different in the Navy, but I didn't know that the Senior Chief, instructor and Recruit Commander, would be another abusive alcoholic.

The first morning, we were rudely awakened at 5 o'clock with flickering bright fluorescent lights and the noise of several tin garbage cans being thrown across the barracks. Next, we heard a string of curse words that would have embarrassed George Carlin. Jumping from our beds, startled and not fully coherent, we stood at the end of our bunks in our underwear, standing at attention as scared as long-tailed cats in a room full of rocking chairs.

I had heard similar curse words many times before from my stepfather, but not with such loudness and conviction. I thought I'd better listen and do to what this son-of-a-bitch had to say. I knew from experience that if I didn't, if I slipped up, I'd get a whipping.

Terrified, I looked up to see who was making all the commotion. I could tell immediately from his flushed face, red bulbous nose, and bloodshot eyes that the Recruit Commander was drunk and angry. He probably came straight to the barracks from a night of binge drinking. I immediately lost any respect for the Recruit Commander. I hated his guts; he even looked somewhat like my stepfather.

"Any of you worthless "pussies" a college graduate?" the Recruit Commander asked with a sneer.

Three brave recruiters, one of them Bob, stepped forward. The instructor slowly took his time and stood in front of each recruit, with his contorted face inches away, and eyeballed each one.

"Alright, which one of you douche bags thinks he can kick my ass?" the Recruit Commander challenged.

Without hesitation, Bob again stepped forward. The instructor again stepped in front of Bob and stared at him eyeball-to-eyeball.

"So, recruit, you think you can kick my ass?" he asked, folding his arms.

"Yes, sir!"

"What did you say, you punk?" the instructor shouted. "Listen to me, dickhead, I work for a living; you address me as Senior Chief not sir, you little bastard."

"Yes, sir....I mean... Yes, Senior Chief!"

"Okay, son, you are the Chief Recruit Petty Officer (RPOC)," the Recruit Commander said in a surprisingly calm voice as he stepped away.

The Recruit Commander along with RPOC Bob chose the rest of the recruit petty officers, including a tall and lanky person who was to be the flag bearer. After the selection, the Recruit Commander gave the first order of the day. "Get your asses dressed and fall in outside to march to the mess hall; you have five minutes."

All the recruits were dressed and in formation in less than the five minutes. "Falling In" was pretty easy; there were eighty circles painted in the correct position to stand on the cement.

In boot camp, recruits didn't just walk anywhere; groups with more than three recruits were required to march from one place to another. Three or fewer recruits had to run. The instructor barked instruction to several recruits who either had a shirt tail hanging out or were slouching, and directed Bob to start the march to the mess hall. Two overweight recruits were commanded to run circles around the formation until they got to the mess hall.

Rarely did we have to stop for traffic because crossing guards were deployed to run ahead and stop traffic as the formation crossed the intersection. After a successful crossing, the guards would run back to get into the formation. After about twenty minutes, the formation halted in front of the mess hall. We waited another five minutes for the Senior Chief to arrive. He walked over and stood next to the RPOC and commanded, "Company, right face; you have fifteen minutes, and fall out!" I was so hungry, I could have eaten the "south end of a north-bound mule." James had written to me about the terrible army chow, and I had heard stories about how much better Navy chow was. So I wasn't disappointed when I saw the bacon, eggs, home fries, and toast. I quickly got into the chow line, loaded up a tray full of eggs and bacon, ate as much as I could as fast as I could, and was back outside in formation in less than ten minutes.

The Recruit Master-of-Arms, Arthur, was a short muscular kid who seemed to be fainthearted. The Senior Chief liked to pick on everyone, but the timid were sitting ducks for him. He was just itching to push Arthur to his limit, but he found out the hard way that Arthur was anything but timid.

One day, The Senior Chief was chewing Arthur's ass about the lack of cleanliness in the head as they walked into the bunk area where the recruits were standing at attention. Arthur opened his mouth to talk back and the Senior Chief raised his hand to strike him. Before anyone could blink an eye, Arthur grabbed his arm, took him to the ground, and stepped on his throat, saying, "Don't do that again if you want to live." When we asked him how he did it, Arthur revealed that he was a martial arts instructor. The Senior Chief didn't retaliate and never bothered Arthur again after that.

Boot camp continued with one class after another: seamanship, firefighting, damage control, and more, but now we were nearing the first of two swimming tests. I was not an excellent swimmer, but I was not afraid of the water as some recruits were. If I passed the first test, then I would be queued to take the second test, but if I failed that, I had to participate in swimming lessons until I passed.

That could extend my time in San Diego, which didn't fit in with my plans.

The day of the swim test was a somber day for some of the recruits, but I wasn't too concerned, since I was a good swimmer. Several recruits were nervous because a sailor had drowned a couple of weeks before as a result of the instructors pushing him back into the deep water when he tried to get out. The first test was to float for five minutes without any floatation device immediately after jumping off a forty-foot platform. The hard part for me was jumping from that height. This practical swim test demonstrated a sailor's ability to stay afloat and survive without the use of a personal floatation device. It was easy, and most recruits passed it. However, the next test was a more difficult test and would cause a number of sailors to be delayed in boot camp or fail. Each recruit was required to swim the length of the pool (fifty yards), then float at the deep end for forty-five minutes, which showed the ability to float indefinitely. We were allowed to use our uniform shirt or pants as a floatation device for the forty-five minute drill. I passed both tests, but, that week, my company lost fifteen recruits. But, at least, no one drowned.

The day after the swimming test was Labor Day. I assumed that, since Labor Day was a holiday, we would have a leisurely day. Boy, was I ever wrong! It was the worse day of boot camp, both for the recruits and for the Senior Chief.

The Recruit Commander started the day in his normal way, but when we returned to the barracks after morning chow we were introduced to, "This is my rifle. This is my gun. This is for fighting, and this is for fun." I grabbed my rifle—I learned never to say gun after the instructor punched someone in the balls who called his rifle a gun—then got into formation. We practiced the drill for the graduation ceremonies for over two hours, which required "beaucoup" marching and exercises with the rifle. Most of the time, we had to shout out, "This is my rifle. This is my gun. This is for fighting, and this is for fun." We were required to sing the words and demonstrate by holding up our rifles on "rifle" and grabbing our crouches on "gun." We marched, went to chow, marched, ate more chow, and marched again and again and again. Just before sunset, with everyone already exhausted, the instructor had us hold our rifles at arm's length over our heads for fifteen minutes, then we had to thrust our rifles from side to side with such force that our hands started bleeding. During one of the fifteen minute holds, one of the recruits, Seaman Apprentice Hebert, dropped his rifle. He picked it up as quickly as he could and resumed the position, but it was too late. The instructor ripped the rifle from his hands, held it with both hands, and butted the recruit in the forehead just above his right eye. Hebert fell to his knees with blood pouring from the gash to his eye. I felt sorry for him and wished that my rifle was loaded so I could shoot the instructor. I thought wryly that it was probably why they didn't give us loaded rifles. Hebert was taken to the hospital, the rest of us returned to the barracks, and the Recruit Commander went home. That was the bloody end of the "leisurely" Labor Day.

The next morning, 5 o'clock passed, then 6 o'clock passed but the Senior Chief didn't appear. I was grateful because we were exhausted. Sometime around 7 o'clock, Chief Mitchell walked into the barracks and called the company to attention. Chief Mitchell explained that Senior

Chief was relieved of his duties, and that he would be our new instructor. He informed us that Seaman Apprentice Hebert was at the Naval Hospital, and after his injury was healed, he would be discharged from the Navy. His injury was severe enough to cause the loss of his right eye. There was complete silence in the room; you could hear a pin drop. I was shocked like everyone else about Hebert. But I was also glad that the Senior Chief was gone and would likely get what was coming to him.

Things improved with Chief Mitchell, he was strict and firm like most boot camp instructors, but he was not a crazy bastard like the Senior Chief. Now, with the Senior Chief gone and swim tests completed, I could see the light at the end of the boot camp tunnel within reach. After another few weeks I would graduate, and head home. Only fifty-three recruits of the eighty recruits who started would graduate, and I speculated that more than one of the twenty-seven dropouts were victims of the Senior Chief. The scuttlebutt was that he was busted down to Chief and sent on a sea duty assignment.

ROAD TRIP

After boot camp, I reported to base for training on November 13, 1969 and checked out one year later on November 13, 1970. I enjoyed living in Millington, Tennessee during that year, since I was a diehard Southerner. I had reservations about going to Miramar, California for my next training assignment on the F-8 aircraft.

My Navy buddy, Corbert, had the same training destination, so we decided to take a road trip from New Orleans to California. Corbert lived south of New Orleans in a small town, Cutoff, Louisiana. Corbert and his family were shrimpers and enjoyed their Cajun heritage with great creole food and parties. Corbert decided he would drive to New Orleans to pick me up and we would drive straight though to Miramar, California in thirty-one hours, taking turns driving every five or six hours. I had trouble sleeping when I wasn't driving and staying awake when I was driving, but we eventually got to our assignment in Mirimar in record time only to find out that the Navy had decided not to train us on the F-8 because the F-8 training was being phased out.

"What the hell!" I told Corbert. "That's no way to run a Navy. What are we supposed to do, sit around and twiddle our thumbs?"

"Well, Joe, I think this here is what my pappy calls the "hurry up and wait" policy. We ain't got much choice but to wait for a new assignment. We might as well look around and find something useful to do while we're waiting."

To pass the time, we decided to work in the fire control maintenance shop to learn general maintenance activities. The reassignment process took the full two weeks before we were assigned to NAS Cecil Field, Florida; this would be our first permanent duty station. Since we were on the West Coast and our new assignment was on the East Coast, the Navy gave us ten days travel time to move to Cecil Field, Florida.

I didn't enjoy the nonstop trip on the way out, so I immediately told Corbert, "We have ten days to get to Florida; that's plenty of time. I don't want to hurry up and wait again. If we get there early, they'll likely not have anything for us to do. So let's plan a more leisurely return trip to New Orleans. We can take four or five days to get there; that would leave plenty of time to pack up and move to Florida."

Corbert agreed. Little did we know at the time that we would need every minute of that time.

We decided to hit the road at 00:00:01 (one second after midnight) because that was the earliest time the military would let us leave the base. Corbert's car was a 1965 Chevelle with a standard transmission, over hundred thousand miles on the engine, and worn tires. I was hoping the car could make one more successful trip across the country without any serious breakdowns.

I decided to take the wheel, as I enjoyed driving at night. We were on the road for several hours and reached the east side of Yuma, Arizona when Corbert's Chevelle overheated. I coasted the car to the side of the highway and stopped as white smoke pouring out from under the hood. It was about 4:00 a.m., dark, and we were in the middle of nowhere. I woke Corbert up.

"Damn, Corbert, your engines overheating and it's only about fifty degrees outside. What gives?"

"I don't know. Not much we can do about it this time of the night. We might as well get some sleep until sunrise and then take a look at it." I readily agreed.

After a few uncomfortable hours of trying to sleep in the cold car, we arose with the sun and started the task at hand. Corbert knew very little about automobile mechanics, but I had observed many automobile repairs while visiting a childhood friend's family of mechanics. Corbert popped the hood and I looked for broken water hoses or belts, then removed the radiator cap to check the water level. The water level indicated that the radiator was not full, but it had enough water. We decided to fill the radiator to the top and run the engine again. After only five minutes, the radiator smoked as it did before. Now I thought that the thermostat could be defective. I removed the thermostat and sealed the connection with water-resistant sealant that I had in my tool box. The engine could probably function well enough without the thermostat. Corbert started the engine and we ran the motor for about ten minutes before resuming our trip.

Corbert drove for several hours while I took a nap. When I awoke, I checked the map.

"Damn, Corbert, we should have stopped in Tucson to get a thermostat and some coolant. What if we get stuck out in the middle of the desert? We better not to take any chances and stop at the next auto parts store. We're somewhere in the Fortuna Foothills with the small town of Gage, New Mexico up ahead."

"Sounds like a good idea," Corbert replied.

We made it to Gage, but there were no parts there and no parts in the next town of Tunis. Fortunately, we were able to find an automobile parts store in Deming, New Mexico. Corbert purchased a new thermostat, new gasket, and a gallon of antifreeze, then I made the repairs. After a little more than an hour, we were on the road again, probably about six hours behind schedule. The Chevelle was running great without any white smoke coming out.

Now, Corbert was driving and I was sleeping in the back seat. We learned that driving in the desert is boring and somewhat stressful. Also, the Chevelle did not have air conditioning which made the heat almost unbearable. Corbert was zoned out when I was rudely awakened by two popping sounds and the car swerving and shuddering to a stop on the side of the road.

"What the hell just happen?" I shouted, jumping up from the back seat.

"I think we blew two tires," Corbert replied nonchalantly.

I got out of the car and found two flat tires, as expected. It was a good thing Corbert had two used tires in the trunk;

he only spent ten dollars for them. We changed both tires and were back on the road again, but I was worried we might not make it to Louisiana, considering the condition of the used tires. We planned to stop overnight for some rest before starting the long trek across Texas. Anthony, Texas seemed like a good place to stop, right on the border of Texas and New Mexico.

Our money was running low, so we decided to stay at the YMCA in Anthony. The YMCA was a dump by our standards, which were pretty low, but for five dollars each, it was the bargain we were hoping for and we happily paid the fee. Then we went to bed for some much needed sleep.

The following morning, we were so hungry, we didn't bother to shower or shave, but walked over to the restaurant for breakfast. We no longer had the buzz cuts from boot camp and we had not shaved in four or five days, so we were beginning to look like a couple of hippies. We ordered some coffee and were looking at the menu when we were greeted by two local police officers, one fat and the other thin.

"Good morning, gentleman, can we see some identification?" the fat policeman asked curtly.

"Sure, officers!" we said as we slowly removed our driver's licenses from our wallets.

"Where you boys headed?" the thin officer asked as they looked at out driver's licenses.

I replied, "Traveling back to New Orleans from California."

"Can we see your draft cards?" The fat officer asked.

For some reason, probably because we were tired and hungry and we were no longer just civilians, we decided to play a joke. "We don't have draft cards, officer," I said.

Immediately, the thin officer put hand on his pistol while the fat one moved closer to us. "You're not registered for the military draft?" he asked.

"Nope!" replied Corbert, opening his wallet again. "But, we do have these cards." Corbert and I handed the officers our military identification cards.

The officers were not amused because they grabbed us by the shirt, walked us over to our car, and made us show them our military orders. This reactions was understandable, considering that it was just two weeks after the antiwar protests in Washington, D.C. where thousands of young men burned their draft cards and chanted, "Hell no, we won't go." After they were satisfied that we were not draft dodgers, we were given a stern lecture about our behavior. Luckily, one of the officer's had a son in the Navy. Otherwise, we probably would have been treated to some jail time.

ATTACK SQUADRON 174

After arriving in Florida, I was assigned to VA-174 for a three-year shore duty assignment. I worked in the organizational maintenance department for about six months, but because of my sharp memory and learning ability, I was assigned to the squadron training department to teach new technician coming into the squadron the A-7A/B radar system, fire control, and weapons system. I quickly became an expert in the Corsair's fire control systems.

After several months of teaching, I got permission to investigate an old APQ-116 Radar Bench that was lying around in a storeroom, and, with the assistance from some of my students, I was able to install the radar bench and incorporate the bench into the radar training session. This gave the students a more in-depth knowledge of the radar systems functionality, which aided them in troubleshooting defective radar systems. Some of my students, Steve, Petty

Officers Kohler and Cathy, and others later became my shipmates during my next sea duty assignments.

Next, I became interested in the Corsair's weapons systems. The A7 A/B weapons used old analog technology, but I was determined to learn how to make this system better and more effective at bombing. I researched the details of the weapons release system and learned that the alignment of the navigation and weapons system was key to the system's performance. Then I began teaching a class on weapon system "bore sighting," which was essential to this alignment.

After getting experience with and teaching bore sighting, I still wasn't satisfied with the performance of the analog computer. After trial and error investigation, I discovered that the analog switch modules could be adjusted to compensate for the time lag in the bombing program. I learned the bombing routines, then documented changes to the alignment procedures to greatly increase the analog bombing system accuracy. I and my supervisors were pleased with this discovery and looked forward to testing the procedures in the next live bombing practice.

JOHN MCCAIN

John McCain, arguably the most famous POW (Prisoner of War) from the Vietnam War, was released from "The Plantation" in March of 1973, where he was repeatedly beaten and tortured by his captors. On his return, John McCain requested returning to flying status, so he endured nine months of rehabilitation to help him physically pass the flight exam. John McCain finished painful physical therapy to be reinstated to flight status in late 1974. Even with the rehabilitation, his injuries left him without the ability to raise his arms above his head.

My first encounter with Commander McCain was when he was the Executive Officer of VA-174 and I was the Petty Officer in charge of the Plane Captains. I supervised about thirty sailors who were tasked with the launch and recovery of the squadron's seventy-five Corsair aircraft. The plane captains cleaned, moved, inspected, fueled, and assisted the pilots, and usually did anything else that needed to be serviced on the aircraft when on the ground.

After making the assignments for the work schedule one day, I noticed that Commander McCain was on the flight schedule for that morning. Most of the plane captains knew the scuttlebutt on him, but we had not met him or knew of his flying status. I assigned Tony Wilson, one of the best plane captains, to his aircraft for that day. Out of the thirty sailors, a third were great workers, a third were okay workers, and a third couldn't care less about the Navy or doing a good job. Since I was new to this position, I wanted to make sure I put the team's best foot forward.

At 1000, Tony and I saw Commander McCain coming onto the flight line. There was no mistake in recognizing him because the injuries he suffered as a POW were plainly visible. His arms were slightly bent and his walk seemed strained. As Commander McCain approached the aircraft, Tony and I stood at attention with a hand salute and welcomed him. Commander McCain returned the salute and handed Tony his flight bag and they begin their flight preparation of the aircraft.

As I walked with them, I said, "You don't have to worry about Petty Officer Wilson, sir; he's one of my best plane captains. Mind if I watch you do the inspection?"

"Not at all," replied Commander McCain.

After they completed the inspection, Tony helped Commander McCain into the cockpit, climbed down to complete the safety checks, and they ignited the engine. After the jet engine starts burning, all communications have to be done with hand signals, as the engine noise is too loud. Standing to the side wearing my sound attenuators for protection, I watched the two complete the flight preparation. I observed as Commander McCain released the overhead safety latch for the injection seat, acknowledged Tony, and then applied power to the engine to taxi his Corsair down the runway.

I continued my relationship with Commander John McCain during his last assignment in the Navy at Attack Squadron One Seven Four from late 1975 to the middle of 1977. Commander John McCain served as my executive officer (XO) and then my commanding officer (CO) where I held positions as Flight Line Supervisor and Quality Assurance Representative. When I was promoted to Petty Officer First Class, Commander John McCain performed my commencement and signed my advancement letter.

There were many rumors and stories about Commander John McCain, both positive and negative, and I decided I wanted to know the truth because my experiences with him were always positive.

He was always polite to officers and enlisted man, using his open personality to promote his ideas and motivate his squadron's men. Junior officers liked him and even assisted him to achieve the carrier qualifications he need. Some senior officers may have disliked him after he was given command of VA-174 without prior commands. Commander McCain's treatment of all personnel was openly friendly, not the standard stiffness, which was not liked by some senior officers. I thought that Commander McCain's promotion was more of a "catch up program" because of his years of captivity in Vietnam, which was considered a normal procedure.

The scuttlebutt was that Commander John McCain had a "maverick" personality, and as a Navy pilot, he liked to "push the envelope." I knew many Navy pilots and I witnessed Commander John McCain's flying ability. So I can say for certain that Commander McCain could push the envelope in an aircraft. But I never knew a pilot who didn't push the envelope; that was a normal attribute of a pilot. I would be worried if a Navy pilot played it safe. "Maverick" is a derogatory term for someone who was an individual, who didn't follow the crowd, but I wondered why being an individual would be a bad thing, especially in a leader.

Another maverick I met was Colonel Harris, a former Air Force pilot who left the Air Force to become a Navy pilot because he wanted to fly off aircraft carriers. The Colonel never seemed to be happy unless he was traveling at supersonic speed and pulling Gs in the sky. The Colonel had the shortest flight preparation known to anyone in the squadron. His demeanor was similar to a Neanderthal looking for a place to piss before killing something. After jumping into the cockpit, he would only make grunting noises for his answers. He followed most normal procedures, but when he acknowledged the catapult officer (the shooter), he would shove a huge cigar in his half-smiling mouth and expose his middle finger to the shooter, as he was flung into the air, happy again.

Another candidate for the nonconformist contest was The Commodore. That wasn't his official rank, but a nickname given him by the enlisted staff because his flying and bombing abilities were far above the highest ranked pilot. Operating in the North Atlantic, his aircraft experienced a "cold cat" shot, a catapult shot that failed to gives the aircraft flying speed. The Commodore immediately ejected before the plane ditched into the frigid waters below, then he parachuted safely back onto the flight deck of the carrier unharmed. The Commodore was on the flight schedule the next morning.

Commander McCain encouraged the squadron to improve its safety record during the same period the squadron worked diligently to increase the aircraft flight readiness. I worked in the quality assurance department, therefore contributed to both program's success by performing maintenance inspections on the Corsair aircraft and assisted with the low spare parts issues. Commander McCain was the best Navy officer and man I ever knew, and I will remember his stories the rest of my life, but Mr. McCain's story of Mike Christian remains close to my heart.

He told it to Tony and me one night after he had returned from a training flight. And at the 1988 Republican National Convention, he told it during his speech.

He said, "As you may know, I spent five and one half years as a prisoner of war during the Vietnam War. In the early years of our imprisonment, the NVA kept us in solitary confinement or two or three to a cell. In 1971 the NVA moved us from these conditions of isolation into large rooms with as many as thirty to forty men to a room. This was, as you can imagine, a wonderful change and was a direct result of the efforts of millions of Americans on behalf of a few hundred POWs 10,000 miles from home.

"One of the men who moved into my room was a young man named Mike Christian. Mike came from a small town near Selma, Alabama. He didn't wear a pair of shoes until he was thirteen years old. At seventeen, he enlisted in the US Navy. He later earned a commission by going to Officer Training School. Then he became a Naval Flight Officer and was shot down and captured in 1967.

"Mike had a keen and deep appreciation of the opportunities this country-and our military-provide for people who want to work and want to succeed. As part of the change in treatment, the Vietnamese allowed some prisoners to receive packages from home. In some of these packages were handkerchiefs, scarves and other items of clothing. Mike got himself a bamboo needle. Over a period of a couple of months, he created an American flag and sewed it on the inside of his shirt.

"Every afternoon, before we had a bowl of soup, we would hang Mike's shirt on the wall of the cell and say the Pledge of Allegiance. I know the Pledge of Allegiance may not seem the most important part of our day now, but I can assure you that in that stark cell it was indeed the most important and meaningful event.

"One day the Vietnamese searched our cell, as they did periodically, and discovered Mike's shirt with the flag sewn inside, and removed it. That evening they returned, opened the door of the cell, and for the benefit of all us, beat Mike Christian severely for the next couple of hours. Then, they opened the door of the cell and threw him in. We cleaned him up as well as we could.

"The cell in which we lived had a concrete slab in the middle on which we slept. Four naked light bulbs hung in each corner of the room. As I said, we tried to clean up Mike as well as we could. After the excitement died down, I looked in the corner of the room, and sitting there beneath that dim light bulb with a piece of red cloth, another shirt and his bamboo needle, was my friend, Mike Christian. He was sitting there with his eyes almost shut from the beating he had received, making another American flag.

"He was not making the flag because it made Mike Christian feel better. He was making that flag because he knew how important it was to us to be able to pledge allegiance to our flag and our country.

So the next time you say the Pledge of Allegiance, you must never forget the sacrifice and courage that thousands of Americans have made to build our nation and promote freedom around the world. You must remember our duty, our honor, and our country."

DROPPING BOMBS

"What's the weather like out there? It's hot. Damn hot! Real hot! Hottest things is my shorts. I could cook things in it. A little crotch pot cooking. Well, can you tell me what it feels like? Fool, it's hot! I told you again! Were you born on the sun? It's damn hot! I said... It's so damn hot, I saw little guys, their orange robes burst into flames. It's that hot! Do you know what I'm talking about? What do you think it's going to be like tonight? It's gonna be hot and wet! That's nice if you're with a lady, but it ain't no good if you're in the jungle..." (Robin Williams, Good Morning Vietnam)

Almost two years had passed before I had the opportunity to test the analog bombing system. I was now in Fallon, Nevada and assigned to VA-46, my first squadron detachment. I was going to test the procedures during the squadron bombing derby. VA-46 pilots would be competing against other squadrons' pilots flying the more advanced

A7-E Corsair with digital computer systems and a Heads-up Display System (HUDS). The HUDS gave the pilots better visibility and ability to use the computer for bombing. Thus, it would be quite a challenge to be able to win this derby.

Practicing dropping "live" bombs preceded our squadron's deployment on the USS John F. Kennedy. There were two places where these activities were done: Yuma, Arizona and Fallon, Nevada, both located in the middle of deserts. Customarily, these detachments involved all the pilots and the designated enlisted personnel needed. Since I was an Aviation Fire Control Technician and weapons specialist, I had the privilege to be included in all these activities. Although the deployments lasted several weeks at a time in secluded locations, there were opportunities for boondoggles with the correct planning. Two of the most memorial ones were a trip to Reno from Fallon and a trip to Tijuana from Yuma.

Everyone arrived early for the Fallon tests, which would include practicing the bombing runs and finishing with a bombing derby against other squadrons. My buddies, Philip and Steve and I had a few days before the planes would arrive, so we planned a quick trip to Reno for some gambling and nightlife before the bombing started. We traveled over the mountain to Reno, arriving around 2200 that night. We drove down the strip and picked the casino with the brightest lights. I loved playing blackjack and immediately went to the tables to play without getting anything to eat. Steve and Philip disappeared into casino's video poker section and I would not see them again unto the next morning.

I played blackjack all night, found Philip and Steve sleeping in the lobby, then we all went to the casino's breakfast buffet. The buffet was the highlight of the trip for Philip and Steve, all you could eat for ninety-nine cents. I think the money the casino lost on food was made up for the gambling done by people who were drawn in by the low price. After they stuffed themselves on the buffet, they would stuff the slot machines with coins. I had won about one hundred dollars, so I paid for the buffet. Most of the morning, we ate and swapped stories about our luck, good and bad. After a catnap, we all decided to gamble till midnight, then hit the road in time to make it back to the base. However, unbeknownst to us, there was a snowstorm brewing.

"Come on guys, we barely have enough time to make it back to base before muster," I said. They agrees, so I jumped in the driver's seat and began our return trip with a bad headache, but we were headed home. Halfway up the mountain, it started snowing hard enough to cover the road. As the tires slipped several times, causing the car to swerve, a concerned Steve asked, "Joe, have you driven in the snow before?".

"Nope, I'm from Louisiana. We hardly ever get snow. I've never seen this much snow before today," I replied.

Phillip said, "Joseph, better let me drive."

I willingly gave the driver's seat to Philip, since he had more experience driving in the snow. We became more concerned as the snow begin to cover the pass over the top of the mountain. The visibility was about five feet as we got to the top of the mountain and thought we would be trapped, but we were able to follow the last snowplow down the mountain to the other side. We made it back to the base in time to take a quick shower, change into our uniforms, and make muster.

Since we had our fun in Reno, I got to work bore-sighting the six Corsairs that were to be used in the bombing derby. I did the procedure over and over again until Philip had to stop me. Next, I adjusted the analog computers to the new specifications that I had developed, then I honed the computer modules to each specific aircraft. One of the computer systems just would not take the programming, so I decided that The Commodore would get this aircraft because he didn't use the computer anyway. The Commodore was so proficient at low-level bombing using only the gun sight, that he didn't need the computer. As a result of my new specifications and detailed work and the skill of The Commodore, our squadron won the bombing derby.

Philip, Steve, and I had never been to Mexico; therefore; on our detachment to Yuma, Arizona, a trip to Tijuana, Mexico just had to be made. We decided to get some beers in a local bar that seemed to be pretty tame. Since Tijuana was close the U.S. border, there were as many Americans as Mexicans in the bar, but not nearly at capacity. To our surprise, the inside was much larger than we thought. Inside the establishment, was a very large bar to the left, dozens of tables and chairs aligned around a stage with a dance floor in front and facing the bar were stairs leading to a second floor. We sat at one of the empty tables and ordered our beers.

More and more partygoers filled the dance floor as the band's festive music permeated the establishment. We were having a great time drinking and watching all the activities when Steve decided that he needed to "oil his gun." We had noticed that some sailors and others would disappear upstairs for fifteen to twenty minutes tops before they would return. We were concerned for Steve's safety, so we kept track of the minutes he was gone. Twenty minutes passed, then thirty minutes, then forty minutes, and still no Steve. I was beginning to get worried.

"Phil, it's been forty-five minutes since Steve went upstairs," I said with concern in my voice.

Phil jokingly replied, "You know how Steve is—very thorough." But I didn't laugh. So to ease my mind, we decided to go check on Steve.

Then we saw Steve as he walked down the stairs with his young lady. They were holding hands and laughing as they sauntered over to the table.

"What's up with y'awl?" asked Steve, sneering.

We joked and talked for several hours before leaving the bar to get some street vendor food and head back to Yuma for the evening.

Before heading back, I checked the outside temperature; it was one hundred and twenty-five degree Fahrenheit in the shade. Although it was hot enough to burst into flames, the feeling was not worse than Louisiana and Florida in upper ninety-degree weather. That's because with the low humidity, you didn't sweat; it evaporated before it could collect on your skin. Still, it was hot, damn hot! The heat didn't do the vendor food much good, and eating it did my intestines even less good.

I wasn't able to get out of my rack for three days except to run to the head down the hall in the barracks. I projectile vomited into a trash can by my bunk, so I didn't have to go to the head too many times. We all ate mystery meat burritos, but I was the only one who got sicker than a dog. Finally, after five days of living on apple juice and crackers, I was able to get vertical and go the chow hall to eat something solid. I made a promise to myself to never eat street vendor food again, well, at least not in Mexico.

The next ten days were constant days of loading live five-hundred-pound bombs and watching bombs explode in the desert. After a few days of these activities, it got somewhat boring. The weapon systems were solid without getting the carrier takeoff and landing pounding, so their maintenance activities were minimal. How was the weather? It was hot. Damn hot! Real hot! Fucking hot!

AVIATION FIRE CONTROL TECHNICIANS

I had gained enough experience to change jobs and become the flight deck troubleshooter for the AQ shop. Aviation Fire Control Technicians (AQs) repair some of the most advanced electronics systems in the Navy. Repair jobs can range from flight deck troubleshooting of the electronic weapon system on an aircraft to changing computer circuit cards in systems components. Aviation Fire Control Technicians perform numerous flight line duties and operate radar and weapon systems in aircraft. Aviation technicians troubleshoot and repair a number of complex electronics systems. Employing all the latest test equipment and procedures, AQs put that training to use repairing systems such as radar, weapons computers, navigation, heads-up display, and weapons-release.

During deployment with VA-46, I had the opportunity to work as an Aviation Fire Control Technician at organizational (shop supervisor and flight deck troubleshooter) and intermediate (bench repair) maintenance. As the shop supervisor, I was the second shift leader for the AQ shop that performed maintenance on the fire control systems. As a flight deck troubleshooter, I was responsible for the operational readiness of the fire control equipment during flight operations as an extension of the AQ shop.

The function of Aircraft Intermediate Maintenance Department (AIMD) is to perform intermediate-level maintenance on all the air groups' aircraft. AIMD on the USS John F. Kennedy was responsible to support the squadron deployed aircraft systems and was usually staffed with personnel from each of the air wing squadrons. I had not been to intermediate-level maintenance training, but I knew the APQ-116 radar system and the fire control weapons system from my instructor days, so I volunteered to work in AIMD for this cruise. Besides, since this was a less stressful bench job, I thought I would be able to use the skills I learned in VA-174.

Already an Integrated Weapons System specialists, I attended Nuclear Weapons Training to learn "wire check" procedures, which would qualify me to supervise weapons system verification on A-7 Corsair aircraft before the aircraft could be loaded with a nuclear bomb. As the leader of the wire check team, I was ultimately responsible for the aircraft readiness.

I had completed these procedures on dozens of occasions with the thought that it was just part of my job. Weapon strategies were changing as I grew more and more concerned about the United States' use of nuclear weapons and my involvement. There was a slight possibility that I would contribute to the deaths of thousands of humans. This troubled me to some degree, but that wasn't the only reason I was having thoughts about leaving the Navy.

I later resolved my personal conflict with nuclear weapons before leaving the Navy. I knew that if it came to nuclear war, I would sign the checklist without hesitation because that was my job and responsibility to my country. I knew very well the nuclear capability of an aircraft carrier, but I kept it to myself.

If a sailor were asked if the aircraft carrier had nuclear weapons or its capacity, they were instructed to say, "I cannot confirm or deny the presence of nuclear weapons."

THE BOATSWAIN'S MATE

"The most versatile member of the Navy's operational team is the boatswain's mate (BM). Boatswain's mates are masters of seamanship and nicknamed "Boats". Boats are capable of performing almost any task in connection with ship's maintenance, small boat operations, navigation, and supervising all personnel assigned to a ship's force. Boatswain mates have a general knowledge of ropes and cables, including different uses, stresses, strains, and proper stowing. Boatswain mates are experts of ship board firefighting and damage control operations. "Boats" skills include knowledge of hoists, cranes, and winches to load cargo or set gangplanks, and stand watch for security, navigation, or communications. Boats are the toughest disciplinarians and hold to Navy traditions."(Wikipedia)

My first encounter with Boatswain's Mate Second Class Schmidt ("Boats") was when I made my way to his berthing compartment to find my rack assignment. I walked into the dimly lit area and found him cutting the buttons off a shipmate's shirt with him still in it, holding him with one hand and cutting with the other hand. He was holding him near his throat and screaming profanities in his face. I was concerned, so I interrupted them.

"Hey, what's going on, Boats?" I asked.

Schmidt looked up at me angrily and groused, "What the fuck do you care, Airedale? This seaman works for me, and I'm just giving him a little motivation."

"I just reported to the squadron and need my rack assignment," I replied. "Are you the master-of-arms?"

He let the sailor loose, telling him, "Don't let me catch you sleeping late again!" Then, turning to me, he said, "Yep, I run this place; if you want anything, you got to come to me."

Boatswain mates are tasked with upholding Navy traditions and making sure everyone follows the rules besides their normal duty assignment. They are usually loud and unorthodox in the enforcement of the regulations, but they also followed the proper protocol in dealing with other sailors. Fortunately, I was two months senior to Boats in the same rank; therefore, I was out of his radar for any of his harassment. We talked and swapped a few stories. I learned that Boats lived aboard a naval ship for most of his eighteen years in the military and probably knew more about a ship than anyone in our squadron (he knew the ropes). He had decided to retire from the Navy as soon as he had his twenty years. We sat at the small two-seat table in our common area and played cribbage until time to get some chow.

Then Boats told me there was an empty rack in the second-class area I could have. The rack was a middle rack and I soon learned that the top rack was better because the middle one was too claustrophobic for me. I was surprised at the cramped sleeping conditions in the berthing compartment, there were over one hundred single bunks, generally called racks, crammed together in stacks of three. The narrow corridors were so small, sailors had to squeeze past each other to pass. Each sailor had an upright locker for clothes and personal belongings, and everybody in the compartment shared a bathroom and a small common area with a television hooked up to one of the carrier's satellite dishes.

I stowed all my gear and tried to get settled into my new tiny space, but I still didn't know how I was going to sleep, sandwiched in between the other bunks. During several months, I became good friend with Steve and Philip and a few other shipmates, and I continued my friendship with Boats. Although Boats didn't show much emotion, I suspected that he enjoyed our time together, despite my being a "fucking Airedale." An Airedale is a naval aviator or any member of the aviation team, officer or enlisted. They're also called "brownshoes." Navy personnel who live on ships (regular Navy) are "blackshoes." Blackshoes usually don't like Brownshoes, but with Boats, I was an exception.

After sharing time together with Boatswain Mate Second Class, I now had a difference opinion along with greater respect for the Boats. As the days of the cruise continued, we learned to appreciate each other's skills, thereby becoming better friends.

WOLF MAN

One of my closest friends was Steve, well known as "The Wolf Man." He was a gentle person with an easy-going personality, a peculiar smile, and one lazy eye. Steve would have been just as comfortable as a hippie on a college campus as being a Petty Officer in the United States Navy. He was another victim of the Vietnam draft, but he didn't have any ill feelings about his situation. He was a "live and let live person."

Steve and I were friends for some time on the USS John F. Kennedy. We met under unusual circumstances. The long hours I had to stand on my feet caused me to get a huge hemorrhoid about the size of a large egg. After treatment for this, I was required to go to sickbay twice a day for several weeks to take siltz baths. There was nothing sacred or private with a bunch of sailors deployed on an aircraft carrier. One day, I was sitting in my bath and across the small room was another sailor, Steve. I decided to strike up a conversation to relieve the boredom.

"How are you doing? I'm Joseph with VA-46.," I said.

"Hi Joseph, I'm Steve. What the fuck are you doing here?"

"I just got here about a month ago when the ship was in Spain."

"I've been on board since the squadron deployed; I'm on temporary assignment to AIMD."

"That's why we haven't crossed paths. I've been here less than a month…now have a bad "'roid." "What are you here for?" I asked.

"A fuckin' spider bit me while I was sleeping, right on the head of my dick! My "gun" got so swollen I had to sit in a tub with an ice pack on my dick till the swelling went away."

I tried not to laugh but failed. Finally I said, "Ouch! That must have hurt."

"More embarrassing than painful," Steve replied.

Of course, Steve was concerned about the bite, but his demeanor didn't show it, as he stayed low key. Steve would be the recipient of spider jokes and stories the rest of the cruise. Probably, there wasn't a day that went by that someone didn't joke about Steve's ordeal, but Steve just rolled with the punch lines.

Steve was a good friend and shipmate, but he had some other talents that would define him as being unique. Sometimes when life got too boring, we would have a contest to help pass the time. The first one was a beard-growing contest. Since there were some who had not shaved in a while, anyone who put in their ten dollars to enter the contest had to shave the day before the start of the competition. All contestants would grow full facial hair for two months, and the one with the best beard or most hair was the winner. Boats was always the final judge because no one wanted to challenge his opinion.

After four weeks, some shipmates dropped out of the contest because their growth just didn't come close to the leaders. After six weeks, there were five of the twenty-four still in the running for the prize money and bragging rights, but when the two months came to an end, the winner was Steve without a doubt. No one anticipated that Steve would be able to grow that much hair on his face, but Steve's beard was so full, he only had two holes for his eyes. From that day forward, Steve was known as the "Wolf Man."

The crew should have known better than to challenge the Wolf Man to a go-without-bathing contest. Steve's abilities were not limited to growing hair but their tolerance for not bathing was. Most contestants gave up after a week and all but Steve quit after two weeks. Steve could beat a Sasquatch in this contest, and his bunk looked and smelled like one slept in it. When Steve finally took his shower, there were twenty shipmates giving him a standing ovation with hopes he would not do it again.

The next contest was not considered a contest to the other sailors, but to Steve, this would be the crown jewel of pranks of all time. Only a few of Steve's close friends knew of his ability to suck blood from his gums. Their berthing compartment had a small area with about four tables with chairs and a television for watching movies. Late one night, there were about fifteen shipmates viewing an old horror movie about vampires and werewolves. Steve was in the front directly under the television with his back to the audience during the most intense scene of the movie. The werewolf had just captured and bit his prey when Steve turned around with blood dripping from his mouth down his beard. He made a growling noise, then, within a few seconds, the area emptied as if the shipmates had been sucked out of the space, except for one sailor who was frozen like a deer in the headlights. Steve looked at him as his blood fell to the deck; the sailor turned pale as he backpedalled across the tables to escape the rougarou-like creature.

In southern Louisiana, the rougarou legend has been spread for many generations by Cajuns. In the Cajun legend, the creature is said to prowl the swamps around Acadiana and Greater New Orleans, and possibly the fields or forests of the regions. The rougarou most often is described as a creature with a human body and the head of a wolf or dog, similar to the werewolf legend.

EDINBURGH

After the USS John F. Kennedy participated in operation Exercise Strong Express in the Northern Atlantic, she stopped in Edinburgh, Scotland for a short stay. I remember that the boat ride to shore was about forty-five minutes long, and I already dreaded the trip back to the Kennedy later that night. Usually, at night, the sea was choppy, which made a very unpleasant ride with stinking, drunk shipmates. As Steve and I were walking down the main street, we discovered a Walgreen's drugstore on the corner, so we went inside to check if the store served food.

To our delight and surprise, there was a serving counter with stools to sit on just like in the United States. All the seats were full, so we waited for two empty ones together. Without any hesitation, we both ordered cheeseburgers, French fries, and cokes with ice, since neither of us could remember the last time we had a burger. When our food arrived, I put ketchup on my French fries, and mayonnaise and ketchup on my cheeseburger, then, with both hands, I hoisted the burger to my mouth. Then, I noticed that the once noisy counter turned almost silent. I glanced up at the other guests at the counter, who were stared at us as if we were barbarians. The other guests had a knife in one hand and a fork in the other. I realized that we were the only ones eating our food with our hands. Evidently, this was not an acceptable practice in Scotland.

Well, we survived our embarrassment, and, in the process, learned how to eat a cheeseburger with a knife and fork. The weather was cold and damp. We just didn't want to go clubbing, so we decided to walk a couple of blocks back toward the launch area and drink some ale at a pub we spotted before taking the boat back to the Kennedy, even though our liberty wasn't over until the next day. The dark, empty pub was without any activity until I looked over to see two young female backpackers enter the building and sit in a booth at the back of the pub. One was a tall girl with short brown hair and just average looks but with enormous hooters. The other was a petite, pretty blond who would barely weigh one hundred pounds soaking wet. I said to Steve, "Let's go over and buy them a beer." Steve was petrified.

"Hi," I said, introducing us, "my name is Joe and this is my friend Steve. We were wondering if you ladies would like us to buy you a beer?"

"Sure, Joe, that's mighty nice of you," said the tall brown-haired girl with a Texas drawl. This here's my friend, Lena. Are you guys sailors?"

"Yeah," I replied, "we're on the USS John F. Kennedy. You girls in college?"

"Well, I was until about a month ago when I ran out of money and had to move back home to Houston. Then I decided to blow what money I had left on a backpacking trip to England and Scotland. I'm getting to be a lot like Lena. She doesn't have any plans for the future; she just likes living in the moment," she said, putting her arm around Lena and smiling.

Both of them looked a little jaded from their travels. Although they didn't verbalize their relationship, we were pretty sure they were a couple.

"Yeah, Rachael and I pooled all our money together to purchase a round trip ticket to London and then backpack across England to Scotland just for fun and adventure. We finally made it to Edinburgh, but our trip took longer than we thought and now were getting low on money. So we really appreciate you guys buying us drinks," said Lena, smiling.

I was thinking that they might be playing us, but they did seem to be sincere. Neither Steve nor I had much money with us anyway, but the beers were cheap, and we enjoyed talking with these Americans. We shared stories and beer with them until early in the morning, when Rachel made a proposition.

"I would love to spend all night talking with you guys, but we really need to find a place to sleep. Do you guys have a room somewhere that you could share with us? Since we don't have much money, we could pay you with… you know… favors."

Steve's eyes almost popped out and fell into his open mouth. I just laughed and said, "Well, even if it wasn't against Navy regulations, I don't think you ladies would enjoy sharing cramped bunks with us. But I think we could help you out. Steve, how much money you got?"

Steve opened his wallet and counted. "I got about twenty pounds."

I grabbed his money, added it to my five pounds and handed it to Rachel, saying, "This should get you ladies a decent room for the night. Thank you for your company. It's been a pleasure."

Steve and I then stumbled to the boat launch. While we were waiting for the next boat, I wanted to talk to my sister, so I called her collect and listened to the operator's conversation on the call.

"I have a collect call from the United Kingdom for Jan, will you accept the charges."

"Yes, I will cover the charges."

"Hi sis, this is Joseph."

"Joseph, why are you at the Magic Kingdom?"

"What? Oh! I'm not in the Magic Kingdom. I'm in Scotland, the United Kingdom."

THE MESS

Enlisted personnel on the USS John F. Kennedy ate their meals in the main galley (kitchen), which could serve as many as 18,000 meals a day. The galley could be called "The Mess" or "The Chow Hall," but not "The Mess Hall" because the Mess Hall was on land. When going to the mess, a sailor is going to get some "chow," but not to get some "mess." Now that should be clear; does anybody know where the "mess deck" is located?

Now, I liked to eat. I lived in New Orleans and loved to eat Cajun and Creole food that are well known in Louisiana, but I ate any good food as long as it was delicious. The quality of a meal on the Kennedy was directly connected to the cooks on board, but more so to the length of time between the periods of replenishment. A good rule of thumb was that if we were any longer than two weeks at sea, then we were in for beaucoup chipped beef meals and powered eggs.

The cooking technology or lack thereof contributed to the food quality. For example, huge boiling pots were used to cook large quantities for meals. But, all in all, the food was good enough as long as the fresh rations lasted. After that, without a replenishment in site, the chow became nearly non-edible. But sailors did have to eat, so they learned to like some of the "waiting for rations" food or may have secretly desired them.

For breakfast, fresh eggs disappeared the quickest and would be replaced with powered eggs, which did not sound too bad until the concoction turned green. If you did not get some powered eggs within five minutes or so, you would then be introduced to, "green eggs and SPAM" or you would have to eat the "creamed chipped beef on toast." The "Red Death" version, like a sloppy Joe mixture with less spice, bothered some, but not me. Another breakfast item was "Dog Vomit," a mealy paste of tomato juice with hamburger and bits of unknowns from a previous meal, usually served on toast. The worst thing for me was the choice of beverages because the powered milk sucked and the main "bug" juice was yellow or green, and I liked purple or red.

Lunch and dinner had the same items available to eat. The Navy had their special version of the Army's shit-on-a-shingle (SOS), only I thought the Navy had better versions—creamy hamburger with peas, creamy red sauce with chipped beef, creamy tuna with peas, or, my favorite, red gravy with hamburger. Although, chipped "beef" was the normal nomenclature on the menu, the meat could have been beef, pork, chicken or mutton. These innovative versions of chipped beef (shit) could be further variegated with the different choices of "shingles"—bagels, biscuits, muffins, rice, casseroles, and, my best choice, home fries.

Some cooks were capable of making a spicy stew similar to gumbo called "burgoo." The recipes varied depending on the availability of leftover items. I often thought about eating at the "geedunk" (junk food bar) when chow deteriorated to this point and hoped the next replenishment would come soon.

The U.S. Navy replenishment at sea was a method of transferring fuel, munitions and stores (food, supplies, parts, etc.) from one ship to another while underway. There were mainly two methods of performing underway replenishment: CONREP and VERTREP.

CONREP – The alongside connected replenishment was the standard methods of transferring fuel, fresh water, ammunition and bulk goods. The USS Kennedy always replenished from the port side of the supply ship (the starboard side of the carrier). Since the ships were streaming close together, a slight steering error on the part of one ship could cause a collision.

VERTREP – Vertical replenishment used helicopters to lift cargo from the supplying ship and lowered the cargo to the receiving ship. There was little risk of collision because the ships did not have to be close to each other, but fuel and other liquids cannot be supplied using this method.

If you didn't care about your chow, then you probably could care less about underway replenishment, but I didn't know anyone who would stay content very long with powdered milk and eggs and SOS.

Although CONREP was required to transfer fuel and other liquids, most were interested when VERTREP was scheduled because it was the primary method to get fresh rations (food) to the galley.

When I worked in AIMD, the conveyor belt passed outside the entrance to our work area. The pallets loaded with boxes were unpacked on the flight deck, then sent down the track to the stores (storage area). We would position one or two men by the conveyor line. Then when an item we needed rolled pass, it was quickly snatched by one of the men and moved to its new location in AIMD. This gave us the ability to enjoy fresh food during low ration periods. Our electronic equipment had refrigerator-cold air piped into cabinets, where ham, cheese, butter and, periodically, some fruit could be stored safely.

We enjoyed ham and cheese sandwiches for lunch and, for dessert, poured honey over bread with melted butter. Thank you for the VERTREP!

YOM KIPPUR WAR

    The Yom Kippur War, otherwise known as Ramadan or October War caused both the United States and the Soviet Union to initiate massive resupply efforts to their respective allies during the war, and this led to a near-confrontation between the two nuclear superpowers. The Soviet Union deployed over two hundred and sixty-five naval vessels in the Mediterranean Sea; most of the ships were supply ships escorted by their combat ships for protection. The United States already had two naval fleets deployed to the Mediterranean and ordered the USS John F. Kennedy and its fleet to return to the Mediterranean just after our deployment to the North Atlantic.

    A U.S. naval fleet usually consisted of forty ships, one hundred fifty aircraft, and twenty thousand personnel. The treaty agreement between the United States and NATO required two naval fleets in the Mediterranean at all times; therefore, with the additional fleet, the United States had three full fleets now in the Med. Although the United States had less ships and manpower, they were all warships, the deployment of these three fleets gave the United States the ability to control the shipping lanes and dominate sea power.

Although the actually war only lasted about twenty days, the air groups were required to maintain air operations for about seventy days. During this period, the United States conducted air operations twenty-four hours a day which consisted of combat aircraft loaded with live weapons. I worked twelve-hour days in immediate maintenance during this period from 2300 to 1100. When I completed work in the late morning, I would read or play card games until lunch time and take a long lunch. After some exercise and shower, I was in my rack by 1500 and awake again by 2200. I maintained this routine for sixty-nine nights straight without seeing the light of day.

The tactic to "hot seat" the aircraft put a beating on the navigation and radar systems on the repeated takeoff and landings. There were times that most of the avionic parts—power supplies, transmitters, gyros, and radar antennas—would fail and require replacement components. I was able to troubleshoot and replace components in the power supplies, gyros and antennas with available supplies on board the ship, but most of the transmitters needed a new magnetron, which was expensive and difficult to stock. I had seventeen of twenty-four transmitters waiting for a magnetron. These defective transmitters put a strain on the operation of the Corsair's radar system that was needed to locate targets and, at times in bad weather, to navigate back to the ship.

YOM KIPPUR WAR

The Yom Kippur War, otherwise known as Ramadan or October War caused both the United States and the Soviet Union to initiate massive resupply efforts to their respective allies during the war, and this led to a near-confrontation between the two nuclear superpowers. The Soviet Union deployed over two hundred and sixty-five naval vessels in the Mediterranean Sea; most of the ships were supply ships escorted by their combat ships for protection. The United States already had two naval fleets deployed to the Mediterranean and ordered the USS John F. Kennedy and its fleet to return to the Mediterranean just after our deployment to the North Atlantic.

A U.S. naval fleet usually consisted of forty ships, one hundred fifty aircraft, and twenty thousand personnel. The treaty agreement between the United States and NATO required two naval fleets in the Mediterranean at all times; therefore, with the additional fleet, the United States had

CECIL SAILBOAT

"ODIN! Now I know,
The secrets of battle,
FIRE! BLOOD and COLD!
When the dust settles!

(Adam Parker)

Chief Cecil was the senior Aviation Fire Control Technician and responsible for running the fire control organization maintenance shop. He had two Petty Officers who ran first and second shifts and Chief Cecil mostly left them alone to run the shop. He was either in the Chief's Mess or the Maintenance Office. He would only come to the shop when he needed to relay some maintenance plans or during ship drills.

Usually, during his unofficial visits, he would share his love of sailing and building his new boat. He had plans to sail around the world after his retirement. He told us about his past sailing adventures with such meticulous elaboration that most of us wanted to scream. Although the Chief was a kind and fair man, we suspected he had been in the Navy too long. I guess our pranks on him were used as revenge for his peculiar behavior and beliefs. One day, Petty Officer Cathy found out about his belief in the Norse god, Odin.

"Sailing alone must be difficult and lonely at times. What do you do if something bad happens and you need assistance?" asked Petty Officer Cathy.

"I pack all the supplies I need, and the boat is rigged so that I can easily sail it by myself. If bad weather or strong seas continue too long, I just call to Odin for help.

"Who the hell is Odin?"

"Odin protects all sailors at sea. I just stand at the front of the boat with my hand cupped on the side of my mouth and call to Odin for help. Odin! Odin! Oh, great Odin of the sea!"

"Un-huh, I see, Chief!"

Chief Cecil was several month away from celebrating thirty years in the Navy. This was quite an accomplishment, but the Navy only allowed a Chief to serve a maximum of thirty years, so his enlistment was in danger of coming to an end. Chief Cecil didn't want to leave the Navy and didn't have any plans otherwise. He completed and submitted a "chit" for special request, asking to stay in the Navy. The reason he gave was, "I, Chief Cecil respectfully request to remain in the United States Navy until death do us part." Chief never departed from his odd behavior, and when word got out about his special request, he was given the nickname of "Cecil Sailboat."

We called him "Cecil Sailboat" only when he was not around. We had a couple of pranks that we enjoyed using on the Chief. Our favorite was hiding the Chief's jacket. When he visited the shop, the Chief would take his jacket off and hang it on the back of a chair. After a few minutes, he would be distracted with some busy work, then someone would hide his jacket. Cecil Sailboat would leave the shop without his jacket and we would return the jacket to the back of the chair. The next time he came into the shop, someone would inform him that he left his jacket there. Chief never realized what was really happening with his jacket.

The Chief wasn't the only victim of our pranks. I didn't have any idea how someone got their "sea legs" (the ability to walk steadily on the deck of a boat or ship and not get sea sick), all I knew was the rough seas and the ship pitching side to side never did affect me. Some of my shipmates, especially the younger first-timers, were very sensitive to this movement. To help them grow sea legs, we would hang a bolt on a string during rough seas—the stronger the seas the more the bolt would swing back and forth from the overhead. The more gullible sailors were encouraged to watch this display, which usually resulted in them turning green and blowing their chow.

FLIGHT DECK
TROUBLESHOOTER

"According to Lloyds in London, working on the flight deck of an aircraft carrier is one of the most dangerous jobs in the world. On the flight deck it is loud, crowded, and the whole atmosphere is often referred to as 'controlled chaos': Jets are catapulted into the air while others are landing, bombs and missiles are transported from the 'bomb farm' to parking aircraft while other planes are taxiing to the catapults or to their parking locations. Even a little mistake can result in an accident: One can be blown off the deck or be sucked into one of the planes' engines. Dangers are everywhere on the flight deck and that is why the people who are working there have to be in perfect physical and mental condition." (www. navybuddies.com)

The USS John F. Kennedy had a large sign on the forward end of the island: BEWARE OF JET

BLAST – PROPELLERS AND ROTORS that reminded sailors of dangers inherent on the flight deck, and the ceaseless vigilance required during flight operations.

Without question, the most dangerous job for an enlisted person was working on the flight deck during flight operations. I had multiple years of aviation training and experience, but there would not be any formal instruction for this job. On my first cruise I worked organizational maintenance in the aviation fire control shop where most of my work was done on the hangar deck, but occasionally I was required to work on the flight deck after flight operations were done for the day. I had heard too many stories and even witnessed sailors being injured or blown overboard, so I decided I would seek advice from Philip and Boats about working on the flight deck.

"Boats, I've been assigned to be the Flight Deck Troubleshooter for the fire control shop. Do you have any advice for me because I'm a little concerned about my safety?

"Yeah, don't do it; it's too dangerous."

"Thanks a lot; no, I'm serious."

"Okay, the first thing is you need to have two mindsets working at the same time: one for safety and one to do your job. Although you have a specific job to accomplish, your primary concern should be keeping yourself out of harm's way."

"How do I accomplish that?"

"The action is too fast for you to be able to think about your job and your safety at the same time, so learn every minute detail of your work activities so you're able to do them in your sleep, then use your awareness for your safety.

If an activity is not that familiar, practice it over and over till you know it.

"That sounds very complicated, Boats...What else?"

"Learn every inch of the flight deck, location of all aircraft and equipment: catapults, elevators and other hazards, and stay away from the arresting gear.

"How do I do all of that?"

"Learning and watching and more learning. There aren't any operations tomorrow; I'll get you started.

"Thanks, Boats; I owe you."

"Fuckin' Airedales!"

I felt better about working on the flight deck and was looking forward to my training with Boats, but I still wanted to talk with Philip because he had done the same job last cruise. Philip wasn't as enthusiastic about helping me as Boats was, not because he didn't want to help, but probably because his method was more from his learned experience and he didn't have to think about it. Nevertheless, I was able to get some good information. His two pieces of advice were like the arcade game of "Frogger" that came on the market in 1981 and similar to the folklore of the Louisiana swamp.

In Frogger, the object of the game was to negotiate your way through multiple moving obstacles without being killed, and you may have six or seven lives to get it done. Many times on the flight deck, you will find yourself in a "frogger" situation, but you only have one life.

Also, operations on the flight deck would become so hectic that it seemed like you were standing in a swamp full of alligators. As Philip put it, "When you're up to your ass in alligators, it's difficult to remember that your initial objective was to drain the swamp."

Being on the flight deck during flight operations maybe a dangerous job, but it was adventuresome one as well. The size of the deck could be compared to three football fields laid end-to-end, only the surface pitched and rolled, then turned into the wind to launch aircraft. Flight operations were done twenty-four hours a day sometimes, so there were differences in the operation during day or night. I thought that night ops were the most thrilling time to be involved with the launch and recovery of aircraft. Usually, seventy-five minutes after the initial launch of the squadron aircraft, a cyclic routine would begin with the Kennedy turning into the wind to facilities this procedure. I would feel the slow motion turn of the carrier, then the wind gradually increased to a steady force as several aircraft circled the carrier in pattern waiting their turn to grab the wire with their aircraft's tail-hook.

Forward of the carrier, "hot seat" activities started as fresh pilots and personnel waited for their opportunity to spring into action. Several Tomcats landed, then taxed forward to quickly change its crew as I watched for the Corsairs to land. Several landed as the pilots and I scrambled to the Corsairs holding area as catapults # 1 and # 2 were ready and their crew shot the two Tomcats back into the sky. One of the returning pilots told me that the radar monitor was not working probably The aircraft needed more fuel and ordinance loaded so replaced the radar display with a new one and quickly tested the radar. Eight minutes later, the Corsair pulled into Cat 1, we pulled all the munitions pins, and the plane was airborne again. I watched the launch as two more of my squadron's Corsair taxied into position.

There were hundreds if not thousands of activities happening simultaneously being orchestrated by the Air Boss, the conductor. If there were not any mishaps or emergencies, then one became part of that day's magnificently directed symphony.

Now, take all of these activities and drop the temperature to twenty degree or below and then be reminded that you would freeze to death in three to five minutes if blown overboard. Boats told me it was "colder than a witch's teat in Idaho." I didn't have any idea what the temperature of a witch's teat was, and I didn't want to find out. I knew I wasn't going overboard. When I was on the flight deck, I knew where to go to escape an emergency and where to bail out if needed. I didn't like to be cold, but staying warm was almost impossible in this weather. I wore long underwear, two pairs of pants, all of my flight gear, wrapped rags around my face and deck coat. Even with all this protection, when the Kennedy turned into the wind, I would feel the cold. We would have to adopt some unsafe methods to not freeze. Of course there were the holding areas to shield you from the wind, but that wasn't always possible. The next method was getting warm from the exhaust of the jet engines. There were lots of those heaters on the deck. You just had to avoid getting too close to them. I soon learned the art of jet exhaust surfing.

FIREFIGHTING

Firefighting training for sailors is essential to the safety of all sailors, and the responsibility belongs to everyone. There are hours of training in boot camp and advanced training is required before sea duty.

Usually, Airedales are assigned with ship's company personnel because they have even more training.

I was not a fan of firefighting nor did I enjoy the training, but I knew it could save lives. I had a justified fear of being burned in a fire. When I was a troubled teen, Geiger gave me the chore of organizing the garage and cleaning the stained concrete floor. After hours of sorting items to store or throw away, I was ready to clean the garage floor. There was an outside faucet close by, so I was able to attach a hose to get water to wash the floor. I used Tide laundry detergent to scrub the floor on my hands and knees.

After I finished the first pass on the floor, I used the hose to rise the floor clean. The floor still looked and felt oily. This wasn't going to[...] noticed a full gasoline can[...] lawn mower. Without muc[...] removed the top and star[...] all over the floor. Then I[...] and spread the gasoline e[...] forgotten the gas water he[...] rear of the garage; I turne[...] a flow of the gasoline rip[...] second later, I heard a lou[...] on my back in the middle[...] on fire!" I screamed. As q[...] through the side open do[...] rolled and rolled to put the[...]

I wasn't aware that th[...] on me. Several minutes pa[...] okay. I glanced back at the[...] burnt itself out. I was all rig[...] luckily avoided a disaster. I[...] thoughts, then completed[...]

This was not the first t[...] but it was the first time [...] myself. My thoughts went[...] French fries on a gas stove[...] fire. But I was able to cover[...] the flames could spread. A[...] matches in the outside stora[...] on fire, but again, I was ab[...] real damage happened. But[...] hurt and causing serious pr[...] Dilton Street when I was pla[...]

[...]good enough for Geiger. I [...]by; I had used it to fill the [...]ught, I grabbed the gas can, [...]o generously pour gasoline [...] the straw broom to scrub [...] across the concrete. I had [...]with a pilot light was at the head just in time to notice toward the heater. A split WOOSH and was knocked [...]he floor. "Oh my God, I'm as this happened, I leaped [...]to a puddle of water, then [...]out.

[...]n continued to pour down before I determined I was [...]ge and the gasoline fire had [...]he garage was all right, and I [...]ed for minutes to collect my [...]ng the garage back together. I had an accident with fire, [...]ne close to badly burning to the time I was cooking the cooking oil caught on [...]ying pan with the lid before [...]er time, I was playing with [...]om, and I caught the garage put the fire out before any [...]losest I got to really getting [...]y damage was the time on with matches in the woods by my house and set the whole woods on fire. I was able to escape the burning grass and make it back home before the firefighters arrived to extinguish the fire. I climbed my favorite tree in my front yard and watched the action in the field from the safety of my lookout.

SICILY

I was assigned to b … a brig runner for one of our shipmates on USS John … . Kennedy's visit to Catania, Sicily. My squadron had … hipmate in the brig serving his nonjudicial punishment … two weeks. During port visits, the squadron was author … d to check out their personnel for work duty in the squ … ron, but only if a petty officer escorted him during this … ignated period. Therefore, I had to remain aboard ship du … g this visit to Sicily.

My friend and shipm … , AQ2 Kohler, had shore patrol duty the last night in Sic … He and his patrol partner were assigned to the nightclub … rea near the waterfront. Kohler was a squared away sailo … ithout a blemish on his record. He and his partner pass … one of the local hot spots and recognized one of the sh … s officer in an argument with a female companion. His … rtner suggested that they leave them alone, but Kohler t … ught that the officer might need assistance, besides he did … have the ability not to intervene.

Enlisted shore patrol were not allowed to detain officers, much less one of the ship's ranking officer.

"Good evening, Sir, do you need any assistance," Kohler said politely.

The officer attempted to stand on his own, but fell back into his chair. It was clear that he was extremely drunk and the woman was his "cruise beau" who traveled to meet with him during port visits. The officer was already aggravated with his girlfriend, but he decided Kohler needed to be served some of his anger.

"Petty Officer Kohler (he had a name tag), can't you see I am busy here with this lady," the officer replied angrily. "Get your ass to shore patrol headquarters and place yourself on report."

"I will deal with you in the morning, Petty Officer." Kohler did as he was instructed by him, but it was a mystery to him what he did wrong.

The widespread stories on the ship about this officer were only thought to be hearsay, and most sailors just wrote them off as pure lies, but Kohler may have stumbled upon more than rumors. This officer was a married man with two young children, but he had a younger girlfriend whom he kept in style and followed the ship from port to port. Another rumor was that the reason for the Kennedy's frequent port visits was so that he could see his girlfriend. On this visit to Sicily, the officer tried to end their relationship, but his girlfriend wouldn't have anything to do with this nonsense. Seems Kohler interrupted their heated discussion and tried to assist him at the wrong time.

Whenever an officer departed or returned aboard the Kennedy, he was always "piped" aboard; therefore, everyone heard the announcement over the ship's 1MC. He came aboard then soon went back to shore after fifteen minutes. I discovered later that he came back to ship only because Kohler pissed him off. Basically, all he did was chew Kohler's ass for trying to help him. Kohler learned a lesson the hard way, but so did this officer shortly after these shenanigans, the officer was relieved of his duties.

THE BELKNAP

"USS Belknap (DLG-26/CG-26), named for Rear Admiral George Eugene Belknap USN (1832-1903), was the lead ship of her class of guided missile cruisers in the United States Navy. She laid down by the Bath at the Bath Iron Works Corporation at Bath in Maine on 5 February 1962, launched on 20 July 1963 and commissioned on 7 November 1964. A guided missile frigate under the then-current designation system, and reclassified as CG-26 on 30 June 1975." (United States Navy)

During the completion of flight operations on November 22nd, 1975 at 22:57 (10:57 PM) the U.S. Navy guided missile cruiser, The Belknap, failed to acknowledge and make course changes that caused the Belknap to collide into CVA-67 John F. Kennedy Aircraft carrier. Immediately the Kennedy severely sliced off the super structure of the Belknap and flushed JP-5 (jet fuel) onto the damaged Belknap. JP-5 was dumped into the storage areas on multiple deck levels on the port side of the ship. The extremely hot fires burned for twenty-one hours and were not completed contained into two days later. The Kennedy's forward catapults (#3 and #4 Cats) were not operational because the fires below the deck warped the thick iron of the flight deck. On board the carrier, a severe fuel fire blazed up the port side, and although firefighters contained the blaze there inside of ten minutes, a receiving room below burned for several hours. At one point, heavy smoke forced the evacuation of all the carrier's fire rooms, forcing her to go dead in the water.

The majority of the firefighting was done by sailors who were trapped or pressed into commission by their proximity to the storage areas. Steve and I were visiting Philip during the "Dog Watch" that night near the port side storage areas. We were only there a few seconds when we heard the collision alert; Philip looked at us and said, "If you want to live, you better follow me." Philip was a more seasoned sailor, who knew the ropes; therefore, we didn't hesitate a fraction of a second to follow his lead.

In less than ten seconds, we slid down three ladders as we had practiced many times in the past. We were one level short of the hangar deck when we heard.

"What the hell is happening"?

In unison we shouted, "Don't stop, and follow us immediately." We descended another level, quickly opened the hatch, and fell onto the hangar deck. As we quickly secured the hatch behind us the inside compartment filled with dark black smoke. Steve and I looked at each other as if to say, "Philip just saved our lives."

Then we heard, "GENERAL QUARTERS, GENERAL QUARTERS, ALL HANDS MAN YOUR BATTLE STATIONS."

We knew this was not a drill. Philip's and my battle station were a firefighting station located near the port side storage areas that were on fire, but we had to find another way to get to that location. Steve's battle station was at a different station. As we passed over the port catwalk to maneuver around the fires, we caught a glimpse of the Belknap on fire about two hundred yards from the Kennedy. Seventy-five percent of the Belknap was on fire and several sailors engulfed in flames jumped off the Belknap into the sea. After seeing this horror, I wondered how anyone on the Belknap could be alive after that.

When we arrived at our battle station, Boats was already there. I was less anxious now, since Boats was the professional and leader of our firefighting team. When the rest of the team arrived, Boats, with firm conviction, commanded us to make ready and don the OBAs (Oxygen Breathing Apparatuses). All of us had practiced in drills many times, but this was not a drill. Boats quickly divided us into two team—one team on the main hose and Philip and me on the second hose, since we had the least amount of experience, and, besides, we were Airedales.

Boats checked the safety of the hatch as both teams entered one of the smoke-filled compartments with no visibility. We heard Boat's voice through the darkness, telling everyone to attach to the safety line. Our mission was to search the compartments, and locate and extinguish any fires. We carried replacement oxygen canisters for the OBAs that were rated to last for forty-five minutes. However, our canisters started dying after only ten minutes. I became alarmed by this discovery and was thinking that I may have been breathing too heavily. I was "ticked off" when I later learned that the canisters supplied from a contractor were defective.

Many hours passed and we only had a few oxygen canisters left. The enormous amount of water being pumped into the compartments caused the water level to rise to our waist level. Boats immediately knew the problem; thus, as he cussed up a storm, he commanded us to find the pumps and remove any sheets or other debris blocking the drainage. In the same breath, he continued to murmur instructions about tying sheets to your mattress. Untied sheets became loose objects that jammed the dumps. We continued our search through storage compartments and even one berthing space close to the fires. The whole team was near exhaustion and nearly out of oxygen when we heard the announcement to discontinue firefighting activities. All of us looked at Boats to wait his instructions; he directed us back to our battle station location. We secured all the equipment and were relieved that we had extinguished the fires and completed our mission. Boats looked at us and said, "Well done, sailors."

After I was dismissed from my firefighting station, I was exhausted and confused, but I slowly made my way to the hangar deck. I wanted to see if I could look out the number two elevator opening to see the Belknap. As I walked onto the hangar deck, the forward section was packed with aircraft and flight deck equipment, an eerie feeling overwhelmed me as I saw seven body bags lined on the deck packed in ice. This somber area was roped off with marine guards who guarded the bodies. I didn't know if these dead sailors were from the Belknap or Kennedy. Visibly concerned now, my eyes began to water, so I moved to my compartment to hide my feelings and check on Steve and other shipmates. That evening an announcement was broadcast that six sailors from the Belknap and one from the Kennedy had died. One sailor from the Belknap was still missing; names would not be released. I could not help but wonder if the sailor I had passed in the black smoke on my escape with Philip and Steve was the dead Kennedy sailor because he was found in the same hallway and died of smoke inhalation. I took a longer shower than normally allowed then fell asleep as tears slowly trickled down my face onto my pillow.

BLACK SANTA

Even with working eight to twelve hours a day during ship duty, there was still a sizable amount of free time aboard ship. I enjoyed playing cards—poker, spades, cribbage, but pinochle was my favorite. Three players can play cut-throat pinochle, which is fun, but the best playing method is with partners.

I had a great pinochle partner, Jarvis; there were very few times that we lost a match. Some pinochle partners used hand signals or voice inflections to push their chances of winning, but neither of these were considered fair card playing. Jarvis and I had worked together for some time and knew each other well; this helped us to read each other. Besides we had a natural style of playing that gave us a definite advantage at playing pinochle partners.

Back in Jacksonville, Florida, Jarvis and I only lived one block from each other. We were both married and had young ones. We were only twenty-four years old with more family commitment than most of our comrades. We talked about our families a lot and we sorely missed them during the Thanksgiving holiday. Two weeks had passed and now we would face Christmas away from home. We planned on play cards as much as we could during the ship's visits in Spain. We also planned a couple of trips on liberty to shop for Christmas presents. During one of our trips, we were walking down the shopping district and noticed a strange object in a store window.

"Look at that suit in the store window. Have you ever seen anything like that before?" Jarvis asked.

"A green Santa suit! No, no I have not," I replied.

"I can see Christmas trees with red and green lights and wonderful bright ornaments, but a Santa dressed in a green suit? Now that's something.

"Let's go into the mall and do some shopping and maybe they'll have a Santa," I suggested.

Joyful holiday music filled the air as we entered the mall to see a giant Christmas tree loaded with ornaments and ribbons in the center of an enormous passageway. Shoppers and families were happily doing their holiday activities just as you might see in a Christmas movie. We saw a long line of children waiting in line with their parents on the other side of the Christmas tree away from us. Our view of the event was blocked by the tree, so we walked over to see what was happening.

As we rounded the tree and moved closer, I saw a large Black Santa Claus dressed in the same type of green Santa suit we saw earlier. I turned to look at Jarvis with a perplexed expression on my face. Then, Jarvis loudly proclaimed, "I always knew Santa was Black."

BARCELONA

My all-time favorite Mediterranean seaport was Barcelona, Spain probably because the USS John F. Kennedy made numerous stops there during my deployments. Besides, the local shop owners and restaurants were friendly to sailors, the streets resembled the French architecture of New Orleans, and the "Los Caracoles" Restaurant delighted my appetite with their Spanish cuisine. On several occasions, I visited the Gothic District near the Las Rambas in Barcelona, and once, on a three-day pass, visited the small coastal town of Sitges with a close female companion.

Several of my buddies and I were finishing our meal close to the restaurant's closing time. We had joked with the wait staff on other visits and they knew we were from the Kennedy. This particular night, the cooks made special appetizers and the servers gathered half-full wine bottles from the tables, then mixed fruit to made pitchers of sangria. The holidays were near with everyone in a festive mood; we ate and drank for hours, laughing and jesting until almost sunrise.

I only had one day before the Kennedy sailed, the liberty launch docked near Columbus Monument on La Rambla, so I knew my location. Los Caracoles was only a short walk north on La Rambla, then two blocks east on Carrer dels Escadellers. I decided I would stop at the United Service Organization (USO) to check on any entertainment events and ask for some information for my next visit before getting some lunch at Los Caracoles Restaurant.

The USO was only a couple of blocks from the port and faced toward the waterfront. I was looking for a quaint little town to visit on my next stop in Barcelona, thinking that a peaceful place on the beach would be great. This cruise came at a terrible time for me, as I was struggling with my past demons, my family situation, and being away at sea on another cruise; I was not making any headway with being away for Christmas. I became more and more distant from Philip and Steve as I had no desire to party and get commode hugging drunk on liberty like most sailor did. Not that I was a teetotaler, but when I drank in this mindset, my sadness only escalated to depression. Philip and Steve wanted to party and smoke hashish that night, and I didn't want to have anything to do with it. Serving time in a Spanish prison was basically a death sentence if you didn't have someone to take care of you. It was too much of a risk for me; I experienced enough of prison visiting my brother at the state penitentiary in Angola, Louisiana. I walked around the USO, drinking a free coke when I bumped into a young redhead near the information desk. She wore dirty baggy clothes, a baseball cap, and had a backpack strapped to her back. Her face was hidden by the backpack as I apologized.

I'm sorry; I wasn't paying attention.

The redhead slowly turned to glance my way. She quickly put her hands over her face and started to cry. "Oh, my God...OH, MY GOD!"

It happened so fast, I didn't have a clue what was going on, and I almost walked away, but I asked, "Is there something wrong? Did I hurt you?"

"Joseph, don't you recognize me? It's Rhea...Rhea !"

Now I had a clue. Rhea was a girl I knew from Metairie. "Hi, hello, Rhea!"

Memories of home flew into my mind. I would have been shocked to see anyone I knew in Barcelona, much less Rhea. I had not spoken with her since we were sixteen. Was she crying because she was happy to see me? Or worse, was she crying because of our past relationship?

Rhea and I lived in the same neighborhood on Christine Street before I moved to my apartment. In junior high school, we rode the school bus together and got off at the same bus stop. At thirteen, Rhea was a chubby, flat-chested girl with a mouth full of braces and a giggly personality. She was pretty with her red hair, but not beautiful. She and I did experiment with kissing and touching, but that was all. I remembered my shredded tongue after our first time kissing. We even had a few dates when we were fifteen, then only a brief encounter at sixteen, the last time we saw each other. Neither of us were sure the reason for this, but I suppose my moving around may have quashed our relationship.

Rhea's family had money from their restaurant business they owned in Bucktown within blocks of Lake

Pontchartrain. I took the bus to her house the last time we were together. We held hands, walking to the levee to watch the sailboats and talk. I believed her parents were strict with her and probably wanted her to date and marry someone of their economic status, but I wasn't sure about that. Although the odds were against our relationship, I wanted to continue to date to see if it would develop. But I returned home after visiting Rhea and we never saw each other again until now.

"Why are you in Barcelona? How did you get here?" she asked, drawing me out of my reverie.

"I joined the Navy when I was eighteen. See that aircraft carrier in the distance? I'm a sailor on that ship."

"You've been in the Navy since high school?"

"Yeah...for almost seven years now. Let's sit over here and talk a minute. I'd like to know more about you."

"Okay." We moved over to the waiting area to talk about old times.

Rhea was a senior at Tulane University in New Orleans, studying art and music. She wanted to go away to school, but her parents paid for her to attend Tulane instead. She explained that she began to really like me, but her parents pressured her to discontinue seeing me. Her parents, especially her father, had an arranged marriage for her with a Greek boy. Rhea wanted to follow a normal American life and shunned the idea of an arranged marriage. This put her at great odds with her parents and other family members. Her compromise was that she would complete college before any thoughts of marriage. Rhea nearly collapsed with fear as she shared her story. She was in Europe for the summer with two of her girlfriends because she lied to her parents about this trip being a requirement for her degree.

Rhea clearly wanted to be with me and asked me to go with her on her trip to Paris, but I knew I couldn't. I explained that the ship would be leaving in the morning and I would be gone for several days, but the ship would be coming back to Barcelona for the New Year's holiday and I would be able to get a three-day pass to spend some time with her. Rhea, with her girlfriends, decided to continue their travel through France to Paris by train and she would return to Barcelona and wait for me. We talked all night into the early morning and agreed on meeting at the USO again. I ran the two blocks and jumped on the last liberty launch back to the ship. Later that night, Rhea boarded her train to Paris. I was thinking I probably would never see her again.

Just as planned, I returned to Barcelona and headed to the USO to find Rhea with a three-day pass in my hands. I entered the building, worried she wouldn't show up, then, when I glanced over to the waiting area where we last sat together, there she was. When Rhea saw me, she stood so I could see her better; she was wearing a lovely fitted blue dress with her beautiful red hair glowing in the morning light. I had not noticed until now how much she had changed. Of course, she didn't have her braces, but she was not the chubby little girl anymore; she had matured into a beautiful woman. I was awed.

As I walked toward her, my ambivalence must have been written all over my face because when I reached her, I paused, and she kissed me on the cheek, posturing to be held. I read her actions and we embraced for what seemed like forever. I was nearly overwhelmed with feelings; I had not been this close to a woman in well over a year. I thought our pass encounters were simply an innocent courtship, but now we both were mature adults. As much as I wanted her, I didn't want to hurt her.

We sat and talked again. Time quickly disappeared into the evening. I suggested we eat dinner at Los Caracoles and take the bus to Sitges in the morning. We crashed at her hostel two blocks away for the night, then jumped on a local bus going south to Sitges. Luckily for us, the bus stopped within a block of our hotel in Sitges. The Hotel Tarramar was a small, romantic place on the beachfront directly facing the Mediterranean. We checked into the hotel, settled into our room, and opened the balcony window to enjoy the lovely beach. We were exhausted from our late night activities and lay down to take a quick nap before doing some sightseeing that afternoon.

We didn't wake up until after three in the afternoon. Now hungry, we took a shower and raced to the town shopping area for a snack. We then strolled along the mile-long beach, holding hands until the sun disappeared below the sea. Our wandering spirits seemed to be at peace as we sat on a bench to listen to the sounds of the tranquil ocean. Rhea opened her heart to me.

"Joseph, I don't have the courage to return to New Orleans. I can't live the life my parents planned for me; my passion is somewhere else."

"Do you have an idea of what you want to do?"

"I believe I want to finish college, then maybe grad school and a career in the art business. I don't want to be married and stay at home."

"Is there a chance you can get your parents to understand your wishes?"

"No, … not at all."

"I thought I wanted to stay in the Navy, to be a lifer. But now, I don't see myself staying in the Navy after my enlistment ends."

"When will that be?"

"Not until 1978, August 1978."

"It seems we are in similar situations."

"Yes, … looks that way."

The evening passed too fast. Almost midnight now, we slowly walked back to the hotel, then went to bed hungry. In the morning, we had planned to get some sun on the beach, but Rhea didn't have a bathing suit and I only had my not-so-sexy Navy trunks. After breakfast, we walked east to find a secluded section of the beach guarded by a mountain cove and we enjoyed our freedom for hours under the sun.

Rhea had an enormous hunger for knowledge that could only be surpassed by her passion for art and music, so we went to the "Old Quarter," where the promenade was decorated with flowers and lined with palm trees. Rhea loved Barcelona, especially Sitges and wanted to see the museums. We walked the small lanes to get to the two museums: Romantic Museum and Cau Ferrat Museum, which were rich with art from Picasso and Dali. Then we strolled the art galleries, and Rhea digested everything in sight. That night, we enjoyed great food, drank incredible sangria, and, for a few hours, we forgot about our families and the unwanted memories in our past.

In the morning, as Rhea and I enjoyed our coffee in silence. We glanced at each other as if we both had the same thoughts. "Joseph…Rhea…." broke the silence in the air.

"Rhea, you go first!" I said.

Rhea declared with conviction, "I am not going back to New Orleans to satisfy my parents' wishes; I will catch up with my friends in Paris and let my parents know my decision to stay in Paris."

"What will you do for a living in Paris?"

"There are several job opportunities that interest me," replied Rhea. You could see the excitement all over her face. "I hope this doesn't disappoint you Joseph," she said, looking concerned.

"Rhea, I think your decision is great and the joy on your face makes me happy, too," I replied. "This cruise is nearly over. I'll stay in Florida for a couple years before my enlistment ends. I want to use that time to complete my college degree, then leave the Navy."

"Joseph, my beloved, will we ever see each other again?" asked Rhea, already aware of the answer.

BEFORE THE EURO

My indoctrination with foreign currency, or, in this situation, European exchange rates was puzzling to me and enjoyable in a way. On my first Mediterranean Cruise, I visited Italy, France, Greece, Spain, and Scotland. This made knowing the dollar exchange rate to Lira, Franc, Drachma, Peso, and Pound somewhat of a challenge but worth the effort. Some sailors called the foreign currency "Beer Ticket" because they had no idea how much the bills or coins were worth. They just wanted to know how many were needed to buy a beer while in port.

Before I departed Naples for my trip to Rome, I exchanged fifty U.S. dollars for nearly thirty-five thousand Italian lire, which seemed to be a fortune to me. I would travel to Rome for three nights and return to Naples and the ship with twenty thousand lire still in my wallet. I spent my half fortune on some souvenirs, eating the great pizza for lunch and, of course, drinking the excellent coffee. The

Italian wine was so inexpensive that it hardly added to my expenses.

Next time, the exchanged currency was to the Spanish peso; I swapped the twenty thousand lire for eighteen hundred pesos. My liberty was short in Barcelona, Spain, but I was glad I got to eat at "Los Caracoles" restaurant that had the best paella and sangria known to man.

I only exchanged twenty dollars for Drachma on my liberty in Athens, Greece. The ship offered multiple tours and I already paid for the guided tour to the Acropolis. I would only need to buy lunch and a couple of beers or maybe a souvenir because I planned to be back on board the ship for supper. I had a chance to try a Red Stripe beer that tasted so bad I dumped it.

Now, all of my currency exchanges seemed to be a "piece of cake" until I got to Scotland, which required using U.S. dollars to purchase items in British pounds. I was told not to exchange on the ship and that most establishments would take the U.S. dollar and credit cards. I had lunch at a Walgreen's drug store sitting on a stool at the counter, same as in the United States. I received the bill for a cheeseburger, French fries, and coke for five and one half pounds, which looked reasonable. However, I was chagrined when I had to pay over twelve U.S. dollars. I was scratching my head on this one; it just didn't seem right. The same meal in Rome would only be thirty-eight hundred lire, which was only a fraction of thirty-five thousand lire and, in Barcelona, it would only be three pesos, which left me with fifteen hundred pesos.

I was pretty good with math, but all of these calculations started to hurt my head. The Euro would be a better idea than I first thought.

BACK HOME

The Kennedy docked in Mayport, Florida at the end of my last deployment, which was nearly two years out of the American way of living. I was glad to be back in Jacksonville with my wife and daughter, but my adjustment would be more difficult than I anticipated. The United States was much different when I departed years ago, and I felt I had returned to another place. I needed some stability to help me adjust to being gone, but even my family seemed like strangers to me. Now, I became anxious because I was overwhelm with unknown possibilities. I took a trip to New Orleans to visit more of my family and some friends, but that only fragmented me more because I had the same empty feeling.

I was having trouble sleeping, and, for months, I lived in an odd space between two different realities, my life during the cruise and my former life before my sea duty. I would think of myself in these two times, and I was not able to live in the present. I was going through the motions until finally, I was transferred to VA-174 to serve the remainder of my enlistment on shore duty. When I reported to my new squadron, they assigned me to be the flight line supervisor. At first, I didn't think this would be a job I enjoyed, but this new adventure turned out to be fun and fulfilling for me. Usually, Fire Control Technicians were not assigned to this job, but I was up to the challenge. In the long run, this job took my mind off of my worries and helped me focus on my life.

Six months passed, then I was promoted to Petty Officer First Class by Commander McCain, thereby requiring me to move to another job. With less duty time, I finished my studies at Florida Junior College, then enrolled in a program to earn a bachelor degree. My focus on my new job and college studies helped me to realize new possibilities. Now, I started to think I had a future as a civilian.

Now that I had some focus, I attended Saint Matthews Episcopal Church in Jacksonville with my wife and daughter on Sundays and developed several new relationships. The church had an active group of men who met for Bible study, but I enjoyed the social time that the group shared: softball, camping, and canoeing trips. I explored kayaking and truly enjoyed these sporting events and the outdoor recreation. Since joining the Navy, I only had Navy friends; therefore, this opportunity helped me develop friendships with some civilians.

The unofficial leader of the men's group was the assistant priest, Robin, not because of his association with the church, but because of his enjoyment of sports and the outdoors. Robin's unorthodox behavior and pastoral abilities allowed him to be a welcome member of the association. Before becoming an Episcopal priest, he studied theatre and performed during his sermons at times, which was not typical of Episcopalians. I liked his "maverick" personality and his love of the outdoors.

One of our planned trips was a weekend trip, which included guided rafting on the Chattanooga River, then kayaking on the Nantahala River the next day. After work on Thursday night, we drove straight through the night to the outdoor center in Tennessee and slept in our trucks the remaining few hours till sunrise. The group enjoyed the rafting and lunch on the river and completed the adventure before dark. We then traveled the short distance from Tennessee to our campground near the Nantahala Outdoor Center in North Carolina. Our campsite had a small stream nearby with a water temperature of forty degree; thus, we were able to chill our beer in the cold water. After a short service in the morning, we started the return trip back to Jacksonville. Everyone was sort of crusty after several days without proper bathing and shaving and we looked fairly grubby. During lunch time, Robin was driving my truck through a rural town with a ham sandwich in one hand and a beer in the other hand. He looked at me, smiled, and said, "No one's gonna believe this is a church outing." All of us were in tears with laughter.

After this wonderful trip, I enjoyed my Navy job, my new friends at Saint Matthew's, and I was able to finish my Bachelor of Science degree. I began to feel connected again and was looking forward to leaving the Navy soon. During one peaceful Sunday afternoon, my daughter asked me to teach her to play hopscotch.

In August 1978, my family and I returned to New Orleans, as I wished to begin a new live as a civilian. With my BS degree, I was able to get an engineering job with Hewlett-Packard Company, and I continued in the Naval Reserves for several years.

CONCLUSION

I left Jacksonville, Florida and the U.S. Navy with a lot more than I started with a decade before. I was married with a wife and two daughters, a college degree, and almost a lifetime of choices and education packed into my naval career. I took my family and my experience back home to New Orleans and welcomed my new civilian life. I carried with me the memories of my many shipmates and adventures, but I will never forget the greatest patriot I ever met—John McCain. I still had painful memories of my early years and even from my Navy cruise adventures, but I was highly optimistic of my future. I was frequently reminded of Rhea, my soul mate, and wondered if I ever would see her again. Many of my friends and others shipmates encouraged me not to leave the military, but I knew that the time had come to move on with my life and the many adventures ahead.

As I received my honorable discharge and set sail for my home, my favorite verse of the Navy song rang out in my mind:

Anchors Aweigh, my boys
Anchors Aweigh
Until we meet once more
Here's wishing you a happy voyage home